WARBONNET CREEK

Center Point
Large Print

Also by E. E. Halleran and available from Center Point Large Print:

The Far Land
Straw Boss
Shadow of the Big Horn
Cimarron Thunder
The Hostile Hills
Crimson Desert
High Prairie

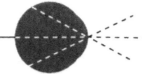

This Large Print Book carries the Seal of Approval of N.A.V.H.

WARBONNET CREEK

E. E. HALLERAN

CENTER POINT LARGE PRINT
THORNDIKE, MAINE

This Center Point Large Print edition
is published in the year 2024 by arrangement with
Golden West Inc.

Copyright © 1961 by E. E. Halleran.
Copyright © renewed 1989 by E. E. Halleran.

All rights reserved.

Originally published in the US by Ballantine Books.
Originally published in the UK by
Hammon, Hamond & Co.

The text of this Large Print edition is unabridged.
In other aspects, this book may vary
from the original edition.
Printed in the United States of America
on permanent paper sourced using
environmentally responsible foresting methods.
Set in 16-point Times New Roman type.

ISBN 979-8-89164-039-9 (hardcover)
ISBN 979-8-89164-043-6 (paperback)

The Library of Congress has cataloged this record
under Library of Congress Control Number: 2023947818

CHAPTER 1

The June sun was still well above the western buttes when Kirby swung the big wagon off the rutted trail. With the ford of Prairie Dog Creek behind him and the big army supply outfit several miles ahead it seemed like a good spot to halt for the night. This might be his last good opportunity to spring that carefully planned trap. He didn't want to spoil the chances by moving too close to the supply train. It was important that Lowry should think him alone and unwary.

Before preparing the evening meal he walked slowly to the top of one of the low rises which marked the rolling country along the North Platte, looking for a distant spiral of dust which might carry its message. Some of the June heat was going out of the day now, and it was good to stretch long legs that had been cramped too long on a wagon seat. Riding that confounded wagon had been the worst feature of this whole program.

Dark eyes skilled in the tricks of prairie observation could still see no sign of movement in the vast expanse of browns and yellows. The country seemed to be completely bare of life. Off to the southeast the green of cottonwoods and willows marked the line of a creek feeding into the Platte, while in the opposite direction Laramie Peak was stark against the sunset. Nearer buttes formed even more distinct silhouettes, but in general the picture was one of vast emptiness. If anyone was watching the Kirby wagon, that watcher was keeping himself carefully out of sight.

Even the guard detail was nowhere to be seen, and Kirby wondered for a moment if the guard had been called off now that the wagon train with its single straggler was getting so close to Fort Fetterman. He didn't quite believe it; the army had been entirely too much concerned about a whiskey trader moving north into country that was upset with the threats of Indian War. They hadn't forgotten him and they weren't neglecting him.

He chuckled a little at the thought. A somewhat tolerant amusement at the army's worry had been one of the lighter features of the past week. He had been under surveillance from the moment he rolled his load of whiskey kegs out of Cheyenne, and at first the army had played it cute. They had kept him with a supply train so that the men watching him could pretend to be the rear guard for the whole outfit. Then, at Fort Laramie, somebody had slipped. He had been allowed to leave the post a full day behind the other wagons—some careful scheming on his part made it seem natural enough. At that point the cat-and-mouse game had begun, the army evidently unwilling to admit that they were watching him.

Suddenly the number of couriers riding the Platte trail seemed to increase amazingly. With so many rumors of trouble to the north Kirby might have been fooled if the army had not made the mistake of using the same men who had come up from Cheyenne as the rear guard. Kirby knew most of them by sight, particularly Sergeant "Alabam" Truitt whose burly figure was as recognizable at long range as his accent was at closer distances.

"I wonder why the sergeant's staying shady?" Kirby murmured half aloud. "He knows damned well that we're not fooling each other one tiny bit."

He smiled a little more naturally at the thought of Truitt's earlier clumsiness and more recent tacit acceptance of their odd relation. Truitt was too good a soldier to admit that he had been assigned to watch Kirby, and Kirby's military background would not permit him to make the sergeant uncomfortable in his duty. They greeted each other in passing and on a couple of occasions Truitt had even halted for small talk, but neither had ever given any hint that they understood each other as well as they did.

In much the same way Kirby had played a game with himself. Now he knew that he wasn't half so amused over Sergeant Truitt as he was pretending to himself that he was. It was just part of his method of keeping himself in some sort of balance. Right from the start he had recognized the danger of permitting a thirst for vengeance to warp his whole being. He had gone out of his way to have active interests completely removed from his main ambition. He had promised himself that a guilty scoundrel was going to be punished, but he did not propose to punish himself by going insane in the process. Vengeance lust could do that to a man.

The promise to himself was part of the reason why he now appeared on a Wyoming prairie, carefully garbed, cleanly shaven and generally looking like a greenhorn trader—which was what he had advertised himself to be. It helped his resolution to play such a role and keep him from becoming too engrossed in grim realities. He forced himself to play the debonair dude because he didn't want the world to see the angry man beneath. And he didn't want that angry man to become the only Mason Kirby.

Now he went at the chore of getting supper. Quickly the dude character slipped away as he shucked out of his frock coat and rolled up his sleeves. With no one watching him Mason Kirby could use his practiced skills to do his evening chores quickly and expertly, his movements deft for a man of his size, with no lost motion. He cooked his meal, ate it, cleaned up his kit, and put it away, accomplishing the entire business before the sun's glare had faded from behind the western peaks. Then, on the chance that somebody might have approached the camp since his first observation, he went back to playing the elegant greenhorn.

He made a sort of ritual of arranging his bedroll beneath the belly of the big freight wagon, and then he strolled idly along the small brook which had been the main reason for his selection of this camp site. At least he seemed to be taking just an idle evening stroll. Only someone directly beside him could have known that those keen dark eyes were watching every creeping shadow of the evening. Tonight might be the night.

There was plenty of reason for his hopes, he knew. His information on the present whereabouts of Joe Lowry had been based on real fact. For the first time since he had started trailing the man, he knew exactly what Lowry was doing and where he was doing it. Plans for baiting him into the open had been laid with great care, but then the Sioux had picked this particular spring to go on the warpath.

"Still a chance," Kirby told himself, again murmuring half aloud. "The way to bait a whiskey runner is with whiskey. I've had the gossip going ahead of me for nearly three weeks so maybe Joe's heard the tale."

What he didn't care to mention to himself was that whiskey was also excellent bait for rampaging Indians. Gossip about the dude whiskey peddler might have carried to the wrong ears. That was a chance he had to take.

"Always seems to be something wrong," he told himself, still using that habit of talking half aloud. "Maybe I wasn't cut out to be a vengeance hunter."

He chuckled in mild whimsy as he said it, but again that was part of his determination to keep his own mental balance. Laughing at himself might help a little, but he knew that deep inside he was just as bitter as he had been that sunny afternoon almost nine years ago when the soldiers had brought Mary's body in to the fort. There would be no rest for him until her murderers were all dead.

He took a couple of quick angry strides along the dusty trail, fighting off the mood and the memories. Then he realized that dusk had fallen rapidly while he paced. It was time to make the real preparations for the night.

From the wagon he produced a second bedroll, a double-barrel shotgun, and an extra Colt's revolver. These he carried to the spot he had already selected, a clear patch several yards away from the wagon and on the opposite side of the trail. From such a spot he would be in a good position to surprise anyone who tried to attack that dummy beneath the wagon.

The possible attacker, of course, ought to be Joe Lowry. By this time the killer must have heard rumors of the greenhorn whiskey peddler. He would very likely have taken pains to follow up those rumors and ought to know that this would be the last night the whiskey cargo would be open to seizure. Another night would see the outfit safely at Fort Fetterman. For Lowry this would be the only chance for the haul he almost certainly would try to make. Kirby could only hope that nothing in the Indian situation would have prevented the whiskey runner from preparing such an attack.

With that final thought he was sound asleep, and the quick chill of evening after the heat of the day made the blankets feel pretty cozy. Falling asleep promptly was a habit he had formed long before starting on his long and baffling search for Joe Lowry. Only more recently had he developed the other knack of waking at the first hint of trouble. He didn't know how he did it, but on many occasions it had stood him in good stead. Somehow he seemed to sense danger when he was asleep better than he did when he was awake. Tonight he felt secure in that ability. If anyone approached his camp he would know it and awaken.

When he opened his eyes again, he saw from the stars that it was just past midnight. There was no moon but the starlight brought the wagon into blurred silhouette, and he could even make out the dark forms of the grazing horses. Far off toward the Platte bottoms a coyote yipped excitedly, and in the rope corral one of the horses shook himself energetically. Otherwise the night seemed compounded of the toneless drone of endless little insect sounds.

After a moment or two of careful listening he decided that his nerves had awakened him unnecessarily. The night was full of nothing but peace. He had been too full of anticipation to sleep. That was all. Or maybe he had made too much of the idea that the danger period would be after midnight. Subconsciously he had set his mental alarm clock for that hour and had awakened without any real reason.

He considered it all half sleepily, and then his keen ear caught a tiny dissonance in the insect symphony. Something not quite a real sound had spoiled the harmony. He didn't know what it had been, but there had been something.

He slid out of the blankets, one hand reaching for the shotgun while with the other he picked up the spare revolver and shoved it into the front of his shirt. Only then did he settle himself to listen for some repetition of the indefinable something which had caught his attention. He was ready. With decent luck he might be about to close out an eight-year pursuit. He hoped so.

After that it became a deadly game of patience, the unknown making slow progress toward the camp while Kirby steeled himself to wait. He knew that the faint sounds were coming from the far side of the wagon, a little to the south of where the horses were beginning to stir in nervous apprehension. Twice a horse snorted in alarm and each time the intruder froze, a long period of flat silence indicating that he was waiting to see whether the horse had awakened Kirby. It was all so slow—and so quiet—that several times Kirby told himself that he was imagining the whole thing. Then a tiny whisper of movement would warn him that imagination had nothing to do with it. Someone was creeping toward the wagon with the utmost stealth.

Suddenly a combination of twang and thud broke the tenor of night sounds. Kirby wanted to swear aloud but restrained himself, not even uttering the grunt of disappointment which came to his throat. Some crazy young Cheyenne buck had tried for a quick scalp, creeping up on the camp and discharging an arrow into what he supposed to be a sleeping man under the wagon.

Still Kirby did not move, only straining his eyes a little more as he tried to find some trace of movement in the gloom. The Indian had not moved after his attack, probably not quite sure that he had disposed of his victim as swiftly as it appeared. He must have been close enough to be sure of the target, but for some reason he was not following it up. Was it because he was not alone? Perhaps Joe Lowry had a renegade partner. Kirby knew that he had to be certain about it; so he held his position and watched for the next move of the murderous intruder.

Then he saw the blur of a dark shadow creeping toward the wagon. The movement was soundless, but Kirby had the fellow spotted this time. The shotgun came up, steadied and belched flame into the night, its boom loud enough to bring an ache to ears that had been straining for the tiny sounds.

It took but a split second for him to roll clear of the smoke and let his eyes recover from the flash of the gun. Then he moved in swiftly, the second barrel ready for action. It was not necessary. A load of buckshot at fifty feet, even in the darkness, was a mighty deadly charge. The crumpled figure near the wagon was motionless, and Kirby had a feeling that the raider had not moved after being blasted to earth by the buckshot. Nowhere else on the night prairie was there a sound except for the stamping of alarmed horses.

Kirby quickly assured himself that the intruder had been alone, and then he lighted a lantern and examined the dead Indian—a young Cheyenne, he knew, and in full war paint. Probably one of the young hellions who were stirring up trouble and trying to taunt older warriors into joining the hostile Sioux. This one had seen what he took to be an opportunity for an easy coup and had sprung the trap intended for Joe Lowry. Kirby had no regrets over killing the Indian; the warrior had tried stealthy murder and deserved his fate. What really mattered was that this would ruin any chance of getting Lowry into the trap. If Joe had been hanging around at all—and now it seemed doubtful—he would have taken the alarm and headed for safer country. This kill-crazy redskin had ruined a lot of things in addition to his own future.

It was now nearly two o'clock, Kirby estimated, so he prepared to get his outfit on the trail. The night had been wasted as far as his main objective was concerned and he knew that he would be too full of annoyance to do any more sleeping. The team had been resting since late afternoon, so it would be just as well to start moving before daybreak. If one painted warrior had ventured to raid the military trail between Forts Laramie and Fetterman, there might be others with similar ambitions. Moving on to Fetterman might prove healthy.

He had scarcely started to hitch up the team when he heard riders coming up the trail from the south. At first they seemed to be moving at a gallop, but as he listened he could hear them slowing their pace. Somebody had been attracted by the gunshot, he figured. They had started toward the scene at a dead run but had slowed to a more cautious pace at sight of the lantern.

For an instant he wondered if he might still get a crack at Lowry, but then he brushed the thought aside. There were at least three of those fellows approaching—and making no attempt to conceal their movements. That wasn't Joe's style.

Still he pulled back, standing in the shadows until the riders became definite silhouettes against the starry southern skies. Four of them, one riding a little ahead of the other three.

He hailed sharply and drew a swift reply. The other man was anxious to make certain that no one around the wagon made any mistakes with a gun.

"Truitt heah," he called, the accent completely familiar. "That yo', Mistah Kuhby?"

The heavy wide-shouldered figure on the lead horse was as readily identifiable as the drawl. Obviously the guard had not been withdrawn but had been simply keeping out of sight.

Kirby grinned in the darkness and replied, "Kirby here. Come on in."

He lowered his voice as the four troopers walked their horses toward the lantern. "Seems like you boys must have been camped pretty close to show up so fast."

"Jest a happen-so, Ah reckon," Truitt told him. "Weall huhd a gunshot and hustled up to find out what it was all about. Have trouble?"

"I *had* trouble. The shotgun took care of it."

He led the way to the body of the Cheyenne, and the sergeant whistled soundlessly through tight lips. "Wah paint, all raht," he drawled. "Looks lahk things ah beginnin' to git mean raht undah ouah noses. Was he by hisself?"

"Seems so." Kirby explained exactly what had happened, omitting only his real reason for having expected an attack on his camp. When he finished, he knew that Sergeant Truitt was staring oddly at him in the lantern's yellow glow.

"Yo' plumb supprise me, Mistah Kuhby," the noncom said in a reproving tone. "Foah a greenho'n that trick o' yo'n sounds real smaht. Ah maht almost think yo' was expectin' some real unwelcome company."

"Why not?" Kirby retorted with a small grin. "You've been on my trail for days."

One of the hitherto silent troopers growled a warning, but the sergeant snapped an order for silence. "Me'n Mistah Kuhby unde'stand each other real good," he said loftily. "He's been a-playin' the greenho'n real smaht, but I'm bettin' this ain't the fust time he's elbowed his way around rough country, mebbe even this heah special bit o' rough country."

Kirby laughed aloud. "Are you really a sharper, or did I play it badly?" he asked. Now that his objective had eluded him, he could relax until some new sort of plan could be formulated. There was no reason why he should not stay on good terms with Truitt. He had come to like the man well enough. The sergeant had inadequate bandy legs under a torso that would have been just right for a heavyweight fighter, but the misshapen body didn't keep him from being a real salty character. He was agile, tough—and apparently a sharp observer.

"Yo' got habits, mistah," Truitt told him. "A man with habits don't hide 'em so good. Ah'd guess that yo've been in the ahmy—but I'd jest as soon not make suah o' the point. It maht tu'n out that yo' was a officeh, and then me and yo' mightn't git along so well togetheh."

Kirby nodded. "So I'm not the greenhorn I've been pretending to be. Does that make me a dangerous character who has to be followed all the time by a squad of cavalry?"

"Raht at the moment it does," Truitt told him, accepting the show of frankness and meeting it halfway. "Yo' ain't got no idea what a ruckus this heah load o' whiskey has been makin'. Mebbe yo' don't know it, but we got ohdehs down heah jest like them generals have got up no'th. They got to find some Injuns and whup 'em. We got to keep another passel o' varmints from bustin' loose wheah they'll need whuppin'. A load o' fiahwateh gettin' into the hands o' them resehvation bucks would suah staht hell to bustin' loose. Mistah Kuhby, yo've had f'm foah to a dozen men jest oveh the hill f'm yo' eveh since yo' pulled outa

Cheyenne. Yo', suh, ah a powdeh keg with the fuse lit!"

"I guessed as much," Kirby admitted. "When do you boys turn back. I'm within a few hours of Fort Fetterman now."

"We ain't a-goin' back. Ouah whole outfit's movin' up to Fettehman in a couple o' days. Supposed to be on hand to suppoht General Crook or General Merritt, whichever gits to needin' some real good men like us. We'll stick raht along with yo' the rest o' the way, long as we understand each otheh so good now."

"Suits me," Kirby agreed. "I'm not sure whether I'm supposed to feel like a favored citizen or a prisoner, but I won't complain. When Cheyennes in war paint start prowling along military trails a man hadn't ought to get too choosey."

Truitt gestured toward the dead Indian. "Supposin' we staht off by fohgittin' all about this vahmint? Lootenint Beckwith's a real rip-snohteh when it comes to wantin' repohts made out."

Kirby grunted his agreement. He had met the pompous young officer in charge of the supply train's escort. Beckwith was probably an efficient commander, but he had not yet discovered that being west of the Missouri had a tendency to make paper work a bit less important. "Save us all a lot of talk," he growled. "Especially me. The lieutenant has not appeared to be one of my more ardent admirers. Not that I blame him too much;

if I was running his show, I wouldn't like the idea of a gent like me trundling a load of liquor around."

Truitt gave prompt orders for disposal of the corpse. A couple of the troopers dragged the Indian to a shallow dry wash and scraped some loose dirt over him, dividing his gear between them as souvenirs. No attempt was made to locate the Indian's pony, and within minutes the wagon was rolling northward with its new escort. Kirby didn't argue about any part of it. He was too disgusted with the way things had worked out. Three months of careful planning, at considerable expense, all blown sky high just because Sitting Bull and some other chiefs had picked this particular year to stir up some hell!

CHAPTER 2

A little past noon they closed in on the rambling fort which had been built at the old crossing of the North Platte. Named for the ill-fated and ill-advised Captain Fetterman it constituted not only a main strong point for protection of travel along the Overland Trail but was also a sort of spearhead stuck into the southern edge of the country the Sioux were trying so desperately to hold. From Fort Fetterman General Crook had advanced toward the Powder with about a thousand regulars and an immense supply train, aiming northward along the eastern slopes of the Bighorns to make a junction with the armies of Gibbon and Terry. Somewhere in the neighborhood of the Powder, Bighorn or Yellowstone they were to use their triple attack to surround the hostiles and herd them back to the reservations they had left during the winter. The first reports from Crook hinted that the Indians were not going to be herded easily.

Kirby stared with interest at the line of low buildings on the immense bluff where Pele Creek came up from the southwest to join the North Platte. It was a big post, a four-company post he had heard, but it was all new to him. Back in the days of the Red Cloud War there had been nothing like a decent fortification between Fort

Laramie and Fort Reno some distance farther north. Reno was still there, but it was merely an outpost now. Fetterman was the center of the projected operation against the Sioux and Northern Cheyennes.

"Ugly, ain't it?" Sergeant Truitt remarked from his saddle.

"Looks strong," Kirby said.

"It ain't. With a riveh and a crick bustin' raht into the middle o' the place we got to keep stock and equipment spread out with wateh in between. The outposts on t'other side o' the riveh could git mighty hot if'n any real scrap stahted up."

Kirby was about to scoff at the idea of Indians attacking such a post, but then he recalled the Cheyenne he had killed during the night. The Southern Cheyennes were still a dangerous factor. Many of their northern brothers were already with the hostiles, Chief Two Moons having led them on the warpath in the early spring. Hotheads were known to be making every effort to take the reservation Indians into the fight, and the danger was so great that General Merritt and his Fifth Cavalry had been patroling the South Cheyenne valley and the southern fringe of the Black Hills for some weeks past. No one knew just how that part of the campaign was working out. It was not too much of a strain on the imagination to think of the Sioux from the Red Cloud Agency combining with some of the Southern Cheyennes to stage a surprise raid on even such posts as Fort Fetterman or Fort Laramie. With the main strength of the army concentrated on the Powder, it would not be bad strategy for the Indian command to try.

Truitt led the way to the edge of the wagon park where Quartermaster wagons stood loaded and ready for whatever move might be required of them. Until the teams were spanned out and the wagon left in what seemed to be a place already assigned to it, no officer appeared on the flat below the fort. Then a stocky rider came down the slope from the main buildings. At the distance Kirby spotted him as an officer, but at first he paid no particular attention. Then two things struck home to him. The officer was a captain and he looked very familiar. John Heilig had put on a bit of weight along with that extra bar on his shoulder, but it was undoubtedly the same John Heilig. Kirby muttered unhappily. Meeting an old friend at this point might prove to be embarrassing.

At first Heilig was cordial enough as he dismounted to shake hands with great warmth and to offer all of the little personal remarks that real friends seem to make when meeting each other after the passage of years. He was not nearly so tall as Kirby but he weighed in at about the same figure, not much of his poundage being fat. He looked fit and hard, with tiny bits of gray showing faintly in his blond hair and mustache.

"I thought it had to be you, Mase," he said, sobering a little. "The name and the description fitted so well even when gossip said you were a stupid sort of green hand."

Kirby tried to pass it off as a joke. "Gossip seems to have been real busy out here."

"We have to keep informed. We've got no picnic around here this spring. When a mysterious load of whiskey comes on the scene, we have to find out a few things. It's my job to find out what the hell you're trying to do."

Kirby shrugged. "Business. What else sells as readily and for such a profit?"

"But why this crazy act of making folks take you for a raw easterner? I'd say you were up to something pretty fishy." He was trying to keep it from sounding too much like a reproach.

"Thanks for asking the question. I'm a bit flattered that you don't assume that this is normal for me."

"Stop dodging. What's the game?"

"When a man is in business he has to get attention or he won't find any customers. This was my way to let people know that I had the stuff to sell. It seems to have worked pretty well."

"You've drawn attention, all right!" The tone indicated that Captain Heilig was not necessarily accepting the explanation even though he didn't intend to press the point just now. He studied

Kirby intently for a few moments and then added, "You've changed, Mase. Not just physically. Actually you look little older than when I saw you last, except for your eyes. Is something wrong?"

Kirby didn't like to have him shooting so close. "Years do things to a man, Dutch. There's a bit of gray around your temples, you know."

Heilig shook his head slowly, and Kirby knew that the light reply had not fooled him at all. Heilig knew that it had not been the years which had changed Mason Kirby. A mere matter of minutes had changed him from a brash young lieutenant—a prospective bridegroom—to a brooding man who had resigned his commission with no word of explanation to anyone. Heilig knew what had caused the change, and Kirby didn't want him to start wondering about how much of the old hurt might remain.

It was Heilig who broke the tight little silence. "I still can't see you as a whiskey peddler, Mase. I heard that you hit it rich in the Montana gold fields. You didn't lose it all, did you?"

"No. I've done all right. In Montana and a couple of other places. But a man needs to keep his capital active."

"By going into the liquor business with an Indian war breaking loose?"

Kirby repeated what he had earlier told Truitt. "There wasn't any war when I started out on this idea. All the papers back east were full of how three nice big armies were going to pacify the frontier in a hurry and open the country for business. How could I guess that Sitting Bull and Crazy Horse were going to put on a big show?"

Heilig lowered his voice significantly even though the enlisted men had moved away from where the conversation was proceeding. "You'd better have a better story than that for the post commander, Mase. I'll tell you right now that the army has picked up some pretty mean suspicions about you. I had a bit of trouble getting permission to talk with you before they tried something a lot more drastic."

Kirby had climbed down now and was facing his old friend at ground level. "Thanks, Dutch, but I think I'd prefer to do battle with the big boys myself rather than to depend on friendship to keep me out of trouble. There never has been any law against selling whiskey out here. I think I can handle the situation."

"Well, your first move will be to start some kind of move to get your property back. My official errand right now is to tell you that the army is seizing it and placing it in a sort of emergency custody."

"What! How do they think they can get away with it? There's whiskey being hauled along every trail in the west!"

"I know. But other wagons are under license, usually to post traders and regular dealers. You're new, coming onto the scene just when everybody is plenty nervous. Now add up a few other facts and you'll understand why this is being done. The army picked up a few facts, you'll understand."

"What facts?" Kirby tried to sound sharp but was afraid that his apprehension would show through. Heilig sounded as though he had picked up a suspicion of Kirby's real errand.

"You want me to tell you what we know about you?"

"Tell me what you suspect. I don't think you know a damned thing. Somebody's got a lot of wrong ideas."

"I hope you're being honest with me, Mase."

Kirby didn't like the sound of that. He had expected embarrassment at the sight of Dutch Heilig; now he was getting it. Deception and friendship didn't go so well together. "What does the army think it knows?" he demanded. "I'll tell you quite frankly whether the guess is right or not."

"Very well. In the first place you've been pretty close to a certain Joe Lowry several times in the past few years. Right?"

"Right." Kirby tried to keep the bitterness out of his voice. That was the frustrating story of the past nine years. He had been *close* to Joe Lowry, but he had never caught him.

"So now this Lowry character is known to be running bad liquor to the Indians. He's been doing it for a year or so, but we can't catch up with him or cut off his supply. We thought we had him over near the Red Cloud Agency, but he gave us the slip. That's his style, switching territories often enough so that he doesn't get caught."

"And what does that have to do with me?" Kirby was still fighting to keep his voice under control.

"We're not sure. But I might as well tell you that last week Nell Perry showed up here at Fetterman. Her explanation for coming into this country alone at such a time is that she recently fell heir to some property which she feels should be shared with a stepbrother she has not been able to catch up with. The stepbrother is Lowry. Incidentally, Nell's staying with Nan and me. Old time's sake, and that sort of thing."

Kirby was staring now. He was puzzled, but at the same time he was relieved. Something in Heilig's tone told him that the officer didn't understand the true situation at all. "Keep going, Dutch," he growled. "You still don't make much sense."

"I'm afraid I do. Nell let slip the fact that several times in the past few years you've met her and been rather attentive. In every instance it was at a time when she was trying to locate this stepbrother, Joe Lowry. Now you show up with a load of whiskey. Lowry's in the region selling the stuff. Nell's right here at the fort. I can't understand a man like you having any dealings with a thug like Lowry, even if he is Nell's relative and even if you may have a sort of eye out for a pretty young widow, but the facts add up kind of nasty. At least that's the official view."

For some moments Kirby didn't know whether to laugh, swear, or simply be astonished into silence. Of all the crazy . . . ! Then he realized what an awkward mess it was. Nell Perry at Fort Fetterman was bad enough in itself. One of the elements in his vengeance campaign which had been most distasteful was the fact that the widow of Perry was a relative of the man he had sworn to kill. Now that she was so close to the scene of possible retribution she might prove to be a serious complication. But sentiment paled into insignificance compared to this monumental piece of bad logic which the army had developed. The idea of Mason Kirby, Nell Perry, and Joe Lowry having some sort of mysterious partnership in the business of smuggling whiskey to Indians was so fantastic that it would have been funny if it hadn't been so maddeningly serious. And Kirby simply could not tell them the truth. The army was the law just now. And the law didn't look with favor on private campaigns of vengeance, even when the law itself had failed.

"You think I'd team up with a piece of scum like Lowry?" Kirby asked after a long pause.

"Normally no. But there seems to be something between you and Nell. A man in love might do some odd things when the lady's relatives are concerned."

"Let's get this straight, Dutch. I'm not in love with Mrs. Perry. It was pure coincidence that I happened to meet her several times recently."

"Also pure coincidence that you always seemed to meet her when she was trying to find this precious stepbrother of hers?"

"Call it that. One way or another, I'm not doing business with Lowry. I never did. I haven't laid eyes on the man ever!" Heilig could not know the real bitterness behind that last statement.

"I believe you, Mase. But I'm afraid the Colonel won't. Officially, I'm still here to inform you that your whiskey has been impounded."

Kirby was glad enough to get the subject changed even to that slight degree. He shrugged a little more amiably. "No worry, Dutch. Actually I never had any particular market in mind for the stuff—and with this Indian war shaping up it's clear that I made a big mistake. If the army wants to store my property for me I suppose I can't complain too much."

"Very well. I'll report that you're raising no objection to the seizure. Now what can I tell Nell Perry? Just between the two of us I have a feeling that she suspects you of having romantic motives toward her. At least she put a bit of something or other into her remarks about the way you keep turning up where she is."

Kirby shook his head. "I'm not chasing Mrs. Perry. And I didn't suspect that she was here at Fetterman until you told me about her. More coincidence."

"Again I'll take your word for it. But maybe Nell won't."

Kirby didn't reply. He didn't like that part of it any more than he liked any other part. Actually it was difficult to decide which factor in the sorry mess was the worst. Indian War, ugly suspicions, Nell, Lowry's getting away again—everything was going wrong.

It was depressing even to think about it. History seemed to be repeating itself. Every time he thought he was getting close to Lowry, something happened to spoil it. It had been that way in Montana, twice in New Mexico and another time in St. Louis. The murderer of Mary Bixler had never seemed to know that he was being trailed, but he always managed to make exactly the proper move to evade the man who had sworn vengeance on him. This time Sitting Bull, a renegade young Cheyenne, the United States Army, and the long arm of coincidence had aligned themselves on the side of the killer.

"No argument," Kirby said finally, remembering that Heilig had actually made a sort of proposition. "It's getting to be pretty certain that this Indian war has busted up my plans completely. Tell the Colonel I'll want a receipt for my property, but otherwise I don't mind a bit if he has the problem of standing guard over a load of firewater."

Heilig nodded in relief. "Which will take some doing," he said with a grimace. "I'll wager that half of the men in the command are planning ways to raid this wagon."

"They're too late," Kirby chuckled. "I think this is the Provost Guard coming to take charge right now."

"So it is. That means we can leave. I've arranged for you to have a room with the post trader while the commander decides what ought to be done about you. Officially he considers you as a trouble maker but temporarily he has agreed to let you stick around as a personal friend of mine."

"Thanks. I'll try to keep from making it awkward for you. Let me collect my gear, and then the guard can start being boss of this outfit. I'll be kinda glad to see the end of it; I don't think I was cut out for the whiskey business anyway." Partly he was expressing a real sentiment and partly he was talking to make an impression. He had to keep Heilig from doing too much thinking on the subject of Joe Lowry. With a bit of luck there still might be a way to get at Lowry, and he didn't want Heilig to know what really was going on.

They climbed the butte together, and Heilig showed Kirby to his new quarters. Kirby was left to give some gloomy consideration to his new status. His mission was a failure, he was suspected of all kinds of villainy on his own account, and he was going to have to face Nell Perry. The act he had used before might wear pretty thin this time.

Two hours later he knew that his prospects were indeed bad. The Indian threat was getting more serious every day and post commanders were tightening regulations all along the line. His chances of getting away to search for Joe Lowry were not very bright.

Hank Weightman, the post trader, brought Kirby up-to-date on the military situation, the florid, balding ex-army sutler showing considerable knowledge of the campaign as well as good insight into what it meant. Billed as a three-pronged offensive commanded by Crook, Gibbon, and Terry it was actually more than that. Merritt's Fifth Cavalry now on patrol along the South Cheyenne had just as important a job as Custer's Seventh up there on the Powder with General Terry. Merritt had to keep the southern tribes from joining the main force of hostiles to the north. His men were in daily fights with small bands, and it was feared that something bigger might break out at any time.

"We got to hope that Merritt can keep 'em

scared," the agent said glumly. "Generals Frye and Forsyth went over to Fort Robinson a spell back for some fancy peace talks, but they didn't get nowhere. The only thing that's keepin' the lid on is the Fifth."

"So far they're doing all right, it seems," Kirby replied.

"So far. If one o' them columns to the north could just get in some good licks at the hostiles, it'd help plenty. Nothing settles Injuns like havin' some o' their friends get the bloody hell beat out of 'em."

"We'll hope for the best."

"And expect the worst. The last report we had from Crook was that he had some real tough opposition ahead of him. If he don't clean 'em out in a hurry, we'll have a dirty mess down this way. A little encouragement is all they need over at the Red Cloud Agency."

Kirby understood the point well enough but he made no further comment. His thoughts were turning to the obvious fact that he probably could not get official permission to travel toward Fort Robinson and the Red Cloud Agency. And, even if he got it, there would be mighty little chance of running down a fellow like Joe Lowry. With Indians stirring up trouble Lowry would probably get out of the region. Once more the long vengeance trail had come to an end.

CHAPTER 3

In the next twenty-four hours Kirby accomplished just one thing. He made a deal with Weightman to handle the wagonload of whiskey on a profit-sharing basis. Major Hawkes, adjutant of the post, was only too happy to get rid of the responsibility of keeping the liquor under guard, and permission was promptly granted to move it to the cellar of the trading post. So long as it was in the hands of a licensed dealer, the army didn't seem to think it worth worrying about.

Captain Heilig stopped by on the following morning long enough to explain that his duties had kept him pretty busy. "Crook's attacking," he announced. "We don't know any details, but he thinks the Sioux in front of him are under the leadership of Crazy Horse. One way or another they seem to be in force."

"You don't seem very hopeful," Kirby commented. "What has happened to the big plan for teaching the hostiles a lesson? If Crook has caught up with them, that's exactly what you wanted."

"Maybe they'll prove too strong for him. We can't afford to lose a fight."

"Sounds odd," Kirby murmured. "Three armies out on the trail. In the old days we were lucky if we could muster a full regiment for a campaign."

"The old days," Heilig repeated. "It doesn't seem possible that it all happened less than ten years ago."

He meant the Red Cloud War, Kirby understood, but there were other things to remember about the old days. For Kirby the starkest memory was of that fine early June day during the peace period which followed the abandonment of the Bozeman Trail forts. Army life had settled down into something like dull routine, and officers had begun to bring their families back to the frontier posts. At Fort Laramie three young lieutenants had planned to join the ranks of the married men, their comradeship making the three separate sets of plans almost a fraternal matter. Dutch Heilig had been the first to bring his fiancée from the east for their wedding, and Helen Lowry arrived soon after to become the bride of Walt Perry. Kirby's bachelorhood had been scheduled to last only weeks longer, but then tragedy had struck. The stagecoach bringing Mary from the railroad had been attacked by bandits who showed their greenness with nervous trigger fingers. They blasted the driver and the coach full of bullet holes, and Mary died in that volley of useless gunfire.

Lieutenant Mason Kirby asked for and received the assignment of taking out a detail on the trail of the killers, but the trio of thugs had made good their escape. That was when Kirby applied for permission to resign his commission.

Heilig changed the subject then as though realizing the kind of bitter thoughts which must have come to Kirby's mind. "We're sending another supply train north tomorrow. General Crook's request."

"But no account of any fight?"

"No. He was preparing to attack some kind of concentration of hostiles on the Rosebud. You don't know that country, do you?"

"Not very well. I know it's along the northern end of the eastern slopes of the Bighorns. North of the Powder."

"That's it. We think Crazy Horse and Dull Knife are trying to keep him from joining up with the other columns. They would know, of course, about the others."

"Trust them to know every move we make. Crook might turn out to be the unlucky one."

"What do you mean by that?"

Kirby laughed shortly. "Don't you remember how all us budding young generals thought we had the Indian War pattern all figured out? Back in the days when we were discovering that Red Cloud could be beaten?"

Heilig nodded, a grin coming to his worried features. "I'd almost forgotten. We were pretty brash, I guess."

"Now you're talking like a captain—and captains don't deal with the higher planes of strategy. They just worry about carrying out the colonel's orders. Only lieutenants know all the answers. Since I never got past being a lieutenant, I can still remember how smart I was."

"Better stay smart," Heilig warned. "Nan wants you to come to dinner with us tonight. As an old married man I think I know the matrimonial gleam when I see it in the female eye. Nan's got a notion that you and Nell are match-making material. Don't say I didn't warn you."

He went out in a hurry, and Kirby was left to wonder at his manner. It sounded as though he had tried to be heavily facetious, but somehow he had not quite brought it off. There had been almost a nervousness behind his attempt at joking.

Weightman, the post trader, had been in a position to overhear the entire conversation so he picked it up quickly. "I didn't know you'd been out here before, Lieutenant. Red Cloud War time, eh?"

Kirby chuckled at the man's quick use of a title. "I'd rather forget it. And I'm not a lieutenant. I haven't been one in a long time."

"Old Red Cloud made it rough," the trader commented. "Spend any time at Fort Phil Kearney?"

"Not during the worst of it. I went in with Colonel Wessels after the Fetterman massacre. Maybe that's how come I thought I knew all the answers. I didn't have to learn them the hard way."

"How'd you figure it?" Weightman asked with a show of interest.

Kirby was willing to talk now. At least he didn't want to let himself think about the Nell Perry angle just at the moment. It had too many complications and life had already become too complicated.

"We decided that only the first campaign in an Indian War would be really dangerous to our side. Indians are emotional fighters. They work themselves up with war dances and a lot of hocus-pocus until they're ready to fight like demons. Then the fighting frenzy wears off, and their natural failings begin to count against them. They don't have the patience or the organization to fight a real campaign. Our formula for fighting the red brother was to let him wear himself out while our side used evasive tactics—then slug him hard when he relaxed."

Weightman nodded. "Sounds kinda smart to me."

"It's not so stupid, even if it's not so simple as we wanted to make it sound. In the Red Cloud War it worked just that way. During the time that our garrison was under siege at Fort Phil Kearney we took a pretty bad beating, mostly the Fetterman business, of course. Then time began to run for us, and the troops made the Sioux look real foolish in fights like the Wagon Box and Hay Field affairs. We didn't have to beat them in a major battle; we simply knocked the enthusiasm out of them after their fighting frenzy wore thin and they went home."

"But the government gave up the ground you won. Tore down the forts."

"Right. We didn't like the idea at all. Of course, they got a deal out of it. The Indians went to reservations—which now they've left again. The Sioux have had eight years to build up a new frenzy, and I've got a sneaking suspicion that the old pattern might show itself once more. If it happens—then General Crook could be right in the spot to be the goat for the tough part."

"We'll soon know," Weightman said shortly. "Ought to be another courier along some time today."

The courier arrived less than an hour later, his message an official secret. However, gossip quickly spread. At Fort Fetterman the story went on the telegraph wires; so it was not long before the news leaked out. The messenger himself could tell little. He had simply carried the story as a relay man from Fort Reno and knew nothing at first hand. General Crook reported that he had attacked a large force of Sioux and Cheyennes on Rosebud Creek. He claimed to have driven them from their defensive position with considerable loss to the Indians. However he had then withdrawn his own force, partly to take care of his casualties and partly because he wanted to fall back on his supply train for more ammunition. He also requested that supplies and ammunition be hurried forward from Fort Fetterman.

Kirby heard plenty of talk, his own experiences warning him that this was not the story of a victory. A commander who had defeated the enemy would scarcely have fallen back. Extra ammunition certainly should have been available for pursuit. But Crook had attempted no pursuit.

Then a second message came in. General Crook was requesting the support of five companies of infantry. Again Kirby could read between the lines. The army pattern had become pretty well established in the annals of plains warfare. For roundup purposes of a chase the idea was to use cavalry. For defense against the slashing attacks of Sioux and Cheyennes the answer was dogged infantry tactics. In the Red Cloud War the defeats had been suffered by cavalry units while the victories had been infantry actions, fought on the defense. It seemed pretty certain that Crook was in trouble.

Kirby rather anticipated cancellation of the dinner date at Heilig's, but just before six o'clock the captain came along to pick him up, a tired smile showing briefly as he said, "I'm finally off duty. Let's go."

Kirby already knew that his old friend was a

supply officer at the post. Heilig would have been busy in seeing that the wagon trains went off on schedule and with the proper loads. Now his work was done and for the present he could ease off a little and let company commanders take over their share of the job.

"We sure did cut the red tape today," Heilig said with apparent satisfaction as the two men walked across toward the line of unpainted frame buildings which bore the falsely impressive title of Officers Row. "Two companies marched today from Fort Reno and another one is divided between the two supply trains as escorts. We'll have two more leaving here in the morning. I think that ought to give General Crook the strength he seems to need."

"Asking for infantry sounds serious," Kirby remarked.

"Likely it is. Anyway you know as much about it as anyone else. The post gossip carries as much of the story as the official reports do."

They dropped the subject there, Kirby silent as he studied the buildings they were passing. Hasty construction and the weathering of the Wyoming climate gave an air of seediness to the area, but at the same time there was something personal here which did not show in any other part of the fort. Curtains at the windows, a few straggling flowers beside doorsteps, the neat row of signs bearing the names of the occupants all hinted at a human element not to be found around headquarters, the barracks, the post store, or any of the other buildings. Here lived people, not mere military accessories.

For a moment Kirby wondered what it would have been like to live with Mary in such a place. Some women never could fit themselves into such a life, no matter how hard they tried. Others settled into the routine and made the most of it.

"Not much to look at," Heilig remarked, as though reading part of his guest's thoughts. "We're a bit more crude here than at some posts, but we make out. All in all we've been pretty happy."

"You were the lucky one."

"I'm sure of it. The Perrys had less than a year to enjoy what they could of garrison life. Then those drunken Cheyennes killed Walt when everything seemed to be peaceful on the frontier. One never knows."

Kirby started to reply but thought better of it. Heilig was not inviting comment but was simply reminding him that there had been other tragedies besides Kirby's. Nell Perry had known her share of sorrow and disappointment also.

They turned in where rows of wildflowers had been cultivated along both sides of the tiny porch, Heilig calling a bluff greeting as he opened the door.

"Look pretty, ladies. Here we come!" He was

trying valiantly to get things off on an easy basis.

His wife came to the door quickly, kissing him and then turning to offer a firm brown hand to Kirby. "You are very welcome, Mason," she said with a smile. "It has been a long time."

Kirby surveyed her with a pretense of being severely critical. Then he let his own smile come. "It can't be so very long," he told her. "You haven't changed a bit. Just as pretty as ever."

Actually he wasn't stretching the point too much. Nan Heilig still had the snapping black eyes which had made her the belle of Fort Laramie, and she hadn't permitted the years to hurt her splendid figure too much. Maturity had added to her charm.

She acknowledged the compliment with another smile and swung away to let him move on into the tiny living room. "You'd better have another nice speech like that for Nell," she told him with a laugh. "I'm sure she deserves it more than I do."

Mrs. Perry had come in from a rear room, offering her own smile of greeting. In contrast to the darker charms of Nan Heilig she was particularly charming with her cool, ash blonde style of beauty. At least two inches taller than the other woman she carried her height well, her figure looking even more youthful than that of Mrs. Heilig. On the frontier many women seemed to run to extremes of plumpness or an especially dry leanness but these two had done neither. Of course, both were still on the near side of thirty, but Kirby had known other army wives who had seemed old at that age.

"No problem in finding compliments for either of you," he asserted. "All a man has to do is have good eyesight and a truthful tongue. Nell, you're looking great."

"Thank you, Mason," the taller woman said quietly. "I'm very glad to see you again." If she stressed the last word a little bit, he could not quite be sure of it. "I was a trifle surprised to hear that you had turned up here as you did, but I'm glad to see you."

"I'm grateful. I came as a sort of disreputable character, I suppose."

"We wondered about it."

He elected to ignore the sober way she said it. "Stop worrying about my morals. I've gone out of business. The post trader bought my embarrassing stock, and the quartermaster was real happy to get a good team and an extra wagon. At the moment I'm in funds and out of the post commander's dog house."

Mrs. Heilig broke in then. "What about you, dear? Will your duties be different now?"

Heilig pretended to misunderstand. "Because Kirby's turned respectable? I don't think so."

"Stop teasing. You know what I mean. Will this business of General Crook's mean that you'll be out on field duty?"

There it was, Kirby thought. The eternal uncertainty of the army wife. He supposed that the Heiligs had been luckier than most, but there was always that nagging worry for the woman who might be left behind at a moment's notice. For Nan Heilig it might even be more of a strain than for the wives of company commanders; she knew that her husband would not be leaving the post unless there was a real emergency. Any move for Dutch Heilig would be a move into danger.

Heilig relieved her concern promptly. "Storekeepers don't have to go out and play hero," he assured her. "I'm just an armchair soldier, and I'm hungry from signing requisitions. What kind of old boiled beef are we having tonight?"

They kept it on the lighter note throughout the meal, no one talking about the Indian war after Heilig made a brief report on what was actually known about the Crook position. In much the same manner they kept away from the subject of Kirby's venture into the liquor business, concentrating on the personal matters which had occupied them during the years of separation. Here the topic was easier for everyone except Kirby, but he managed his share of it without getting on to particularly dangerous ground. His search for Joe Lowry had taken him into many parts of the west, but each time he had gone as some sort of business man and his various exploits were worth relating. Partly because he had never caught up with Lowry he could tell his story without mentioning the man he had trailed for so many months.

Even with the care he had to exercise—and with the realization that Heilig was watching him intently—he found it rather easy to forget the variety of bad luck which had hounded him recently. He had feared that this meeting with Nell Perry might prove extremely awkward, but it had not turned out that way at all. She was friendly, even cordial, but she did not turn the conversation into the channels which Kirby had dreaded. He could simply enjoy being with her.

It was only when the evening was drawing toward its close that this pleasant state of affairs lost some of its charm. Then it was Nan Heilig who opened the way for tension, her remarks about the Indian troubles suggesting that she had been thinking about them all the time that she was putting on a gay show of being the perfect hostess.

"Be honest with us, dear," she begged her husband. "Do you think that General Crook was defeated up there on the Rosebud?"

Heilig didn't try to evade the direct question and once more Kirby found himself thinking that this was the way it had to be with army wives. They knew when to suspect trouble, and there wasn't much point in trying to fool them about it. Probably the women of Officers Row had threshed the whole matter out during the afternoon with as much insight as any of the staff at headquarters. After all, it was a matter of grave personal concern to every one of them.

"We're afraid he took a bit of a beating," Heilig admitted. "No real disaster, of course, since he's preparing to move forward once more, but enough of a delay so that the Indians will probably consider it as a victory for them. That's why it may prove to be serious for some of us down this way."

His wife nodded. "You think the Indians at the Red Cloud Agency will take to the warpath with that kind of encouragement?" Obviously she understood the situation quite thoroughly.

Her husband hunched his shoulders just a trifle. "That's why General Merritt has the Fifth over there. It's a risk we've had to consider from the beginning."

"And General Merritt has already had to do some fighting?"

"A little. Patrol actions. The last reports were that things were reasonably quiet. When the first malcontents found themselves getting chased back to the reservation, it had a good moral effect."

Mrs. Heilig was persistent. Having brought up the subject she wanted it made clear. "But there will be a change in Indian morale if they think the hostiles in the north have won a victory. Isn't that right?"

Kirby broke in with a laugh that he was afraid would sound as forced as he knew it to be. "You're determined to learn the worst, aren't you? Wait until we know more about this Rosebud fight before you start worrying."

"I'm worried already," Nell Perry stated calmly. "I came up here because I had excellent reasons to think I would locate my stepbrother at or near the Red Cloud Agency. Now it appears that I may not be able to make the trip to that point. The army has funny notions about letting women travel into what it considers dangerous country."

"Smart army," Kirby said shortly.

"And I'm worried about Joe too. I understood that he was in some sort of business deal with the Indians at the reservation. I'm afraid his business will be interrupted even if he is not in personal danger."

"We're making inquiries for you," Heilig said, shooting only the briefest of side glances at Kirby. "If we learn anything, we'll let you know. If it seems safe to permit you to travel to Fort Robinson, I'll see to it that you get a pass. You might as well stop fretting about it."

"Don't sound so stern, Captain Heilig," she retorted with a smile. "I know I'm a lot of trouble to you, particularly at a time like this, but I can't help being anxious about Joe."

49

There was an awkward silence as the Heiligs exchanged glances. Kirby knew what it meant, but before he could find some way to work in an innocent sounding question Mrs. Perry broke the silence, obviously trying to restore the good humor which had so suddenly vanished.

"I suppose I'm due to be frustrated again," she complained. "This makes the fourth time I've almost located my stepbrother. Each time I thought I was about to catch up with him and each time the same thing happened. I ran into Mason Kirby instead. Mr. Kirby, I think you're a bad luck omen for me."

She made it sound wryly humorous, but Kirby found it difficult to play up. He was all too well aware that the Heiligs were listening intently, that odd look passing between them once more.

"I'm hurt," he said with an exaggerated frown. "Just for that I'll go back to my quarters and listen to the snoring of my friend Weightman. The partitions in that place make him sound like he was right in the room with me."

They broke it up then, joking in a somewhat restrained fashion as Kirby made the usual thank-you speech. Finally he was out in the darkness of the night, wondering just what it was that the Heiligs had been thinking. Clearly they must have some ideas about Joe Lowry. He hoped they hadn't gotten any new ones from that remark Nell had made.

CHAPTER 4

The night was a restless one for Mason Kirby. Weightman's snores seemed to be louder than ever, but it was Kirby's thoughts that were really keeping him awake. For one thing he kept puzzling over the odd behavior of the Heiligs. Dutch had probably told Nan about Lowry's liquor smuggling when Nell first appeared at Fort Fetterman. It was official knowledge, of course, and might well have been passed along to an army wife. But did the Heiligs know or suspect anything more than that? Could they have any possible hint that Joe Lowry was the last surviving murderer of Mary Bixler?

Finally he decided that the important facts were known only to himself. The Heiligs were simply worried because they could see Nell getting into a spot where she would be hurt. They would have liked to save her the knowledge that her stepbrother was a particularly vicious type of border thug. Kirby could sympathize with that viewpoint; he had gone to quite a lot of trouble to keep her from learning the whole truth.

After his first two unexpected meetings with Nell he had taken careful account of stock, asking himself why he should not tell her about Lowry. The answer bothered him. Nell was much too physically attractive and had a fine sense of humor. He was afraid he might well fall in love with such a woman. And that wouldn't do at all.

Each time that Nell came into his thoughts—and that was pretty often—he tried desperately to make himself think along other lines. He had to make plans. What would be his next move? Would there be any next move? He had ample funds, both here and available for draft. Somehow he ought to be able to get around this Indian situation long enough to follow up his real objective.

He slept in snatches, each time rousing to the knowledge that confused dreams had plagued his brief slumbers. He didn't mind the Cheyennes in war paint who kept uttering war whoops which sounded suspiciously like Weightman's snores. What bothered him was the way his dreams kept confusing Nell Perry with Mary. Finally it bothered him enough so that he found himself wide awake, his mind suddenly analytical on the subject. For nine years he had carried a sort of dream picture of Mary in his mind, a picture which had never been too clear. Actually they had been childhood sweethearts, never very close to each other after they grew up. It had been a sort of correspondence romance. The letters from a budding young lieutenant on frontier duty probably appealing to an impressionable, romantic girl back in Rhode Island. Kirby knew now that he had proposed, by mail, to a girl he had known only as a child. Heilig's marriage and Perry's engagement had set a sort of romantic pattern for him, a pattern which had proved to be one of heartbreak and bitterness. Probably he and Mary would have been happy together, but he was beginning to wonder whether he had ever been in love with her. In all probability both of them had simply been in love with the idea of being in love.

It was a fine time to reach such a decision, he told himself. After nine years of dedicating his life to a grim crusade of vengeance he was realizing that he hadn't really been in love in the first place. Not that it made any difference in a way. Mary's murderers had to be punished and no one knew who they were. No one except Mason Kirby, of course.

When he opened his eyes after finally going into something like sound slumber, he knew that the day was well advanced. Outside he could hear the normal sounds of military post activity, and he knew that subconsciously he had been hearing other sounds from time to time. He knew that those two relief companies had marched out shortly after reveille. He had a feeling that the post was reorganizing for replacements from the south, fatigue details active in place of regular drill. A man who had learned military routine thoroughly could recognize familiar sounds even in his sleep.

When he finally managed to get himself out of bed and through the chore of shaving, he knew that he would have to make a move. There was nothing to keep him at Fort Fetterman except the military embargo that had been placed on civilian travel. His deal with Weightman could be worked out at a later date, and meanwhile he had only his saddle horse and his personal effects to encumber him. Maybe he could manage to get clear of the place and stalk Joe Lowry from a different angle. What he had thought about Mary during the night made no difference; Lowry had to pay the penalty.

Accepting a cup of coffee from the post trader, but refusing any belated breakfast, he moved out into the hot morning sunshine, studying the activities of the post. Almost immediately he spotted Sergeant Truitt in charge of a loading detail. Wagons had been brought up from the lower plain, and ammunition was being transferred to them from the magazine.

"More calls for help?" he asked Truitt as he moved into watch.

"Nope. Cunnel jest plays it cute. If he gits a call he'll be ready fer a fast move."

"Smart," Kirby agreed. "Any more word from General Crook?"

"Nope. Had a rideh in f'm the Fifth this

mohnin'. Even kinda quiet oveh thataway. Could be things ain't as bad as they looked."

"Your outfit arriving from Laramie soon?"

"Mebbe today." The burly man grinned. "Got real good duty this time. The boys is eschotin' the paymasteh. Makes 'em slow but we ain't complainin'."

Kirby decided that this would be a good time for him to inspect the fort. With the paymaster coming and so many other bits of business to occupy the official mind he should be able to study things out without too many people realizing what he was doing. If he planned to leave the place without permission of the post commander, he needed to know how it would have to be done.

It did not take long to discover that the only good possibility would be the back trail. The confluence of the Platte and Pele Creek made some sort of ferry job imperative to anyone moving out in any direction except to the south. But that would be all right. Perhaps he could get permission to make a return toward Fort Laramie. Probably they'd be only too glad to get rid of him. Once clear of the fort he could find some way to take the direction he really had in mind.

He ate a substantial meal with his new landlord, discussing in general terms a possible belated settlement on the whiskey deal. By that time he had come to the conclusion that Weightman was a pretty substantial character. It would be fairly safe to trust him for the amount owed. Anyway it wasn't important. Money was not the object.

They were just finishing their meal when a hail from somewhere beyond the main buildings indicated the arrival of the paymaster and his escort from Fort Laramie. Kirby went out immediately, curious rather than really interested. Obviously a lot of other people had the same kind of curiosity for the parade ground seemed to be well populated, everyone moving across toward the edge of the bluff which commanded the lower ground to the southeast. Off-duty enlisted men, a few officers, wives, laundresses, teamsters—they were all out to look.

Three women were coming toward him as he moved out into the open, and at first he didn't realize that any of them were familiar to him. Then one left the others and came straight toward him. It was Nell Perry, a light summer print dress displaying bare arms and shoulders. Somehow he had not noticed last evening, but now he was pleasantly aware of the smooth tan which seemed to contrast so well with her blondeness. So many women went to great pains to preserve the whiteness of their skins that it was a little unusual to see one who let the sun do things for her. Even the wide brimmed hat was little more than an eyeshade as she wore it.

"May I walk with you, Mason?" she asked when she was within earshot.

"My pleasure. I'm sure I couldn't find a prettier walking partner on the post. On the whole frontier, I should say."

"Thank you for the compliment. Coming from you it's especially gratifying. I don't think I ever heard you offer one before."

"An oversight, I'm sure. The material has been available all the time."

She took his arm and they turned toward the area where the others were congregating. "This is exasperating," she said with a little laugh. "For the first time I catch you in a gallant mood and I have to spoil it by asking some serious questions."

"Forget the questions." He was afraid he was a little hasty with it.

"But I can't. Last night—and again this morning—the Heiligs did a great deal of talking about Joe. They asked a number of questions which sounded odd to me. I don't think they really asked the questions they wanted to ask, but I can't imagine what they were really driving at."

"Why ask me?"

"Because it all started while you were with us last evening. Something must have been said that started them off. Did you ever meet my stepbrother?"

"No." He was glad that he could be truthful.

Probably he would have to do some lying before this business was over, but at least he was honest so far.

"Are you sure?"

"Positive." Again he could be truthful, utterly truthful. He had never seen Joe Lowry even though he had spent eight years trying to do so.

"I simply don't understand it. I'm sure the Heiligs were interested in that remark I made when I joked about finding you instead of Joe every time I looked for him."

Kirby decided that this might be a good time to dispel some of Nell's illusions about her unsavory relative. Break the news gently, so to speak, and at the same time get this talk away from more dangerous angles.

"How much do you know about Joe?" he asked quietly.

She looked up at him, hazel eyes appearing dark against the pale hair which swept down on her forehead. "Now you sound like the Heiligs. Is something wrong with Joe?"

"Answer my question. Then I'll answer yours."

"Very well. I don't know him at all. My father married Joe's mother when we were children. I was ten, I believe, and Joe was fourteen. He ran away from home when he was sixteen, and I don't really remember him very well. I never heard from him again until just after I came out here to marry Walt. I got word that he was coming west and would stop in and see me. I waited for months but he never appeared. We were at Fort Laramie then and much later I heard a rumor that Joe had been in Cheyenne, but he never came to see me."

Kirby didn't tell her why. Lowry and his murdering companions had left the territory in a hurry after that stagecoach business. It had taken Kirby months of painstaking detective work to figure out the identities of the guilty men, but he had done it. Now only Lowry was left to pay the overdue penalty.

She went on quietly, "About a year after Walt—died—I came into a little property from my father. He left it to me, but I felt that Joe was entitled to share in it. That's when I started trying to locate him." She uttered that little laugh again as she added, "You know the rest of it. I seem to miss him all the time."

He knew that she was recalling her joking remark of the previous evening, the one which had apparently caused the Heiligs to do some thinking. "Then you haven't actually seen him in all these years?"

"No. And now I'm beginning to wonder. As I look back on it I seem to recall that wherever I asked about him people were pretty evasive. I'm hoping that you'll be honest with me. Is there something wrong about Joe that I don't know about?"

"I'm afraid there is. That's why the Heiligs acted the way they did. They didn't like to hurt you by telling you what they know of him."

"But I want to know."

"I said I'd answer your question. The army has been trying to catch him for several months. He has been running liquor illegally to the Indians at the Red Cloud Agency. There's at least a hint that part of the trouble there was stirred up by his whiskey."

"And before this? He has had a bad reputation?"

"Yes. I think a lot of strangers have tried to protect your feelings just as the Heiligs seem to be doing."

"Thanks for being frank with me."

He tried to steer her away from the more dangerous ground. "Actually I have an interest. When I came up here with a load of whiskey, there were folks who believed that I intended the stuff for Joe. There has been a broad hint that you were in on the deal. When you said what you did last night about finding me where you expected to find Joe I'm afraid the Heiligs started to wonder. You'd better set them straight."

"But it's ridiculous! I don't . . ."

"I know how you feel. I was just as flabbergasted when Dutch Heilig told me that the talk was going around. I'm hoping that it'll end now that I no longer have an interest in that particular line of work."

A distant column of horsemen appeared then and they watched in silence, neither of them paying too much attention but simply using the sight as an excuse for silence. It was clear that Nell Perry didn't quite know what to say. Kirby was willing to let it go. He was afraid that any more talk might get him into subjects he preferred to omit.

It was many minutes later that Nell murmured, "I can't get over it. There are just too many coincidences involved."

"It does seem that way."

"And if I feel that way about it how will other people feel? I don't think we can ever convince the Heiligs that there hasn't been something between us that we're keeping secret."

Again Kirby had to steer the talk away from dangerous ground. "Maybe we should tell them that I've been pursuing you because of romantic interest. They'd believe that, all right."

"Why should they?"

"Why not. You're a very attractive woman. Any man with eyes might make a play for you."

"You didn't."

"How do you know? Maybe I'm just too shy to admit it. Or I have been until now."

"Please don't try to make jokes now. I think this is serious."

He wanted to tell her that he was entirely willing to make it serious, but he knew well enough that he could not. A man can't make love to a woman at the same time that he's planning to kill her relative. So he simply said, "It is still a possibility for satisfying the Heiligs."

She nodded, not too happily. "I suppose it is. How do you propose going about it?"

"Spend the afternoon with me. Go back to Heilig's place a bit late and put on the girlish confusion act. Let Nan worm the story out of you that you and I have been getting pretty chummy, that I've finally admitted chasing you around the country all these years. Maybe even ask to have me to dinner again. I'm tired of Weightman's cooking anyhow."

She smiled in some amusement, but her voice grew serious as she told him, "You'll have to remember that we'll just be playing our parts. Don't try to take advantage of the arrangement."

"I'll be tempted."

"You're talking nonsense again. I shall remember that you never paid any attention to me until something quite impersonal made it suit our mutual convenience. Naturally I'll not be flattered at knowing that fact, but I'll keep it in mind. You must do the same."

Again Kirby had to say something far different from what he would have liked to say. "We understand each other," he told her. It was better to let it go than to let himself get tangled any deeper.

"Very well. Then we'll play it right up to the hilt. You're invited to dinner again this evening. I'll tell Nan and apologize for being swept off my feet. She'll understand—or she'll think she does."

"Sounds nice."

"Careful." Then she smiled a little more easily. "But not too careful, of course. We'll try to make it look good, and we might as well get some fun out of fooling people. Life's too serious anyway."

That was a sort of keynote for the afternoon. Nell was going out of her way to be gay and charming, a job which she did with notable success. At least Kirby thought so. They wandered around the military post, looking at everything and occasionally comparing arrangements to others they had known at other establishments. Nell had known only about a year of garrison life, but the year had been enough for her to learn a great deal about it. They could talk about a great many common interests, only occasionally getting into areas where painful memories for one or both would be involved. Then it always seemed that the other one recognized the danger area and quickly changed the subject.

The sun was getting low in the west when Nell finally suggested that they make their next move. "I think we've stirred up enough gossip for one afternoon. Probably I won't have to be much of an actress when I meet Nan. She will have heard about us from a dozen tongues by this time."

"I'll be around to dinner," Kirby told her with a chuckle. "If the evening turns out to be as pleasant as the afternoon did, I won't have a bit of trouble in playing my part. You make it mighty easy for a man."

"I've enjoyed myself also," she told him quite frankly. "It's almost too bad that we're only play-acting." Then she added quickly, "Very well! So I'm being unladylike about it. Just remember that poor widows have to be a bit more frank than the sweet young things."

"Poor widow, my foot! You . . . But never mind. You gave me orders."

He walked with her as far as the end of Officers Row but left then to turn back to the post trader's. At first he felt pretty good about the way everything was turning out, but then something like sanity began to return. He had made a mess of the whole business, he knew. Instead of keeping entirely clear of Nell Perry he had ventured into an arrangement which would almost certainly become more complicated. He couldn't deceive himself into thinking that he was not strongly attracted to her, and she had hinted quite broadly that she would have welcomed real attention from him. Just because he wanted a way out of a temporary embarrassment he had let himself get into a position where he would be using her good will for a pretty nasty purpose.

For a few minutes he considered sending some sort of lame excuse to her and stopping the whole sorry business. Then he realized that by now she would have started passing her hints to Nan Heilig. If he let her down at this point, it would be almost as bad as whatever might develop later. The only thing to do was to play the game through temporarily and let her know that he was going to get away from Fort Fetterman. He didn't know how that would be accomplished, but he couldn't plan on staying around any longer. Matters were going from bad to worse.

CHAPTER 5

The dingy bar room which served the post as an unofficial Officers Club was buzzing when Kirby left his own quarters. The restraint of the past few days seemed to have dissolved, and at first he assumed that it was merely a matter of men anticipating tomorrow's payday. Then he caught enough of the talk to know that several messages had come in, all of them good. There had been no additional word from General Crook's camp along the slope of the Bighorns, but General Merritt was asking to have his regiment recalled from the patrol duty on the South Cheyenne. Matters were quiet there, and it seemed evident that the tribesmen at the Red Cloud Agency had decided to stay clear of the northern troubles. A group of the older chiefs had gotten control and were bending every effort to keep the peace.

In a roundabout way there was a good word from Terry. His column, marching west from Fort Abraham Lincoln, was now in Sioux country, Sitting Bull's main concentration reported just ahead. Custer and the Seventh Cavalry were scouting in advance to locate the hostiles so that Crook's opening attack could be followed up by a joint blow to be delivered by Terry's and Gibbon's forces.

"It could be all over by this time," a bronzed captain declared to a pair of young lieutenants. "The fight on the Rosebud was on the seventeenth and today's the twenty-fourth."

"Twenty-fifth," one of the lieutenants corrected.

"Right. Out here it's easy to lose track of dates. Anyway I've got a feeling that better news is on its way right at this moment."

Others seemed to agree. The back of the Indian uprising was broken. There would be mopping-up operations but no real campaign. It was obvious that the thought came as a relief to the older men but a disappointment to the young ones. For Kirby it suggested a way out of his difficulties. Major Hawkes, the post adjutant, was just leaving the place so Kirby hurried to overtake him.

"Excuse me, Major," he said with careful courtesy, remembering the adjutant's tendency to be a bit self-important. "I'd like to get permission to travel toward Fort Robinson with the paymaster's escort. I imagine you're the proper officer to see about it."

Hawkes stopped short, suspicion showing in the narrowed black eyes behind their shaggy brows. "For what purpose?" he demanded. "You must be aware that civilian travel is restricted and that you have been subject to considerable scrutiny."

"I understand. I was so unfortunate as to take

a fling at the liquor business at just the wrong time, and some odd coincidences made it appear that I might be doing something illegal. But I've sold not only my stock but also my team and wagon—which you may recall was bought by the army. I have no reason to remain on this post as I do have a sort of personal errand at Fort Robinson."

When the major hesitated slightly Kirby followed it up. "Perhaps Captain Heilig has told you that I formerly held a commission and that I was a scout officer for some time in this area. I know the valley of the South Cheyenne quite well, and I understand that you are a bit short of civilian scouts who are properly acquainted with it. I'd be glad to serve as a volunteer for the one trip."

Hawkes's frown eased a little then. "You seem to be pretty well informed on matters, sir. But you're correct. Now that the situation seems to be a trifle less critical, I think our restrictions might be relaxed. And we are somewhat shorthanded where civilian scouts are concerned. So many trains going out have almost stripped us of competent men, and General Merritt took every man who knew the least bit about the valley of the South Cheyenne. I think we might come to an understanding, sir."

"Very good, sir. A sort of exchange of courtesies might prove mutually helpful."

"Be ready by noon tomorrow, in case Colonel Stanton is ready to move by that time. I'll take the matter up with the commander."

Kirby thanked him again and hurried away. He felt a little better now about going to dinner at Heilig's. For one evening he could play the game without getting himself tangled too deeply—he hoped. Meanwhile he could brace his resolution with the knowledge that there was still going to be a chance for him to track down the elusive Joe Lowry. He knew that he still had to carry out his vow, no matter what happened afterward. He would simply have to make certain that he did not see Nell Perry again—ever.

In spite of his satisfaction at this new turn of events he could not help but be surprised at his reception. He had expected that Nell would carry out some of the campaign she had outlined. In the afternoon she had talked as though she wanted to make the Heiligs think of her as a woman suddenly and madly in love. But she made her greeting almost impersonal and Kirby was left a bit at a loss, not knowing how to react. He fell back on a careful politeness and the others followed suit, the meal turning out to be a moody sort of affair. Heilig tried to keep the talk on the better morale of the post, but no one followed it up.

Finally Kirby asked, "Is something wrong around here? I'd rather be accused than to feel that I'm condemned without my knowledge of what I'm getting blamed for."

"Who said you were being blamed for anything?" Nan Heilig replied.

"I just had a feeling."

"And correctly," Nell broke in. "We weren't going to bring it up until dinner was over, but I suppose there's no point in delaying any longer. Do you believe that my stepbrother killed Mary?"

It was the question Kirby had expected the least. So far as he had ever been able to determine, no one had suspected the true killers of Mary Bixler. It had been his private fight and he had never even hinted at the truth to anyone. Now the question came out bluntly.

His astonishment and perplexity must have been apparent because Nell demanded, "Have you been using me as a means of catching Joe?" Her voice was not quite so steady in this second question and he knew that she was having trouble in keeping herself under control. There seemed to be no possible reason for delaying the issue now, but he still fought off telling the facts.

"Where did all this crazy business come from?" he asked. "Why should you think I would try to use you for any kind of underhand purpose?"

"Because I'm afraid that's exactly what you've been doing."

"Let me get into this," Heilig broke in quietly. "A matter such as this one is bound to get pretty emotional, so perhaps it would be better if an outsider took charge for a few minutes. Do either of you mind?"

"I don't," Kirby told him. "Just so I find out what is going on."

Nell simply shook her head.

"Let me go back almost nine years," Heilig began. "Mase, when you left the army so hastily, we were worried about you. You must realize that you had not been yourself at all after Mary's death. We were afraid you might do something foolish, so we arranged to keep an eye on you. When you went over to Cheyenne, we passed the word to a couple of friends at Fort D. A. Russell and they assumed a sort of guardianship. We weren't really attempting to spy on you, but we found out what you were doing. We also managed to piece out the information you must have received—simply by following your trail and talking to the same people you had visited. We felt sure that you had worked out a pretty good case for identifying the murdering bandits, but that it was not a case that would hold up in court. At that point you disappeared and we didn't know where you had gone."

"May I hear what that case was?" Nell asked in a low voice. "Our talk before dinner didn't get that far."

Kirby knew that he had been the subject of some pretty unhappy talk within the past hour, but he was more concerned to know just how far Heilig would be able to call his shots. He had an uneasy feeling that his little secret had not been so much of a secret after all.

Heilig didn't look toward Kirby as he went on, "We think that Kirby picked up a clue here and a hint there until he was pretty sure that the three men who staged that fatal holdup were three loud young fellows who had lounged around the town for almost a week but who had ridden out on the trail to Fort Laramie several hours ahead of the stagecoach. Hours before any word reached Cheyenne about the holdup this trio came back to town, sold their horses and gear, and climbed aboard an eastbound train. By the time that scouts had learned that the holdup had been the work of three men and had tracked them back toward Laramie, it was much too late to find out where they had gone. No one knew their names or anything about them. The conductor of the train didn't remember them. Both civil and military officials went to work on what we found, but it was no use. We had no way of identifying any of them, and we didn't know whether Kirby was on their trail or not.

"Another thing occurred to me then, but I didn't tell anyone else about it. I happened to remember that Walt Perry had told me that his brother-in-law was on his way west and would stop to visit them. A little later Nell mentioned that she was disturbed because her stepbrother had not appeared even though she had had a second note from him saying that he would reach Cheyenne on a certain day. I wondered if he might have been one of the bandits. The time fitted exactly.

"Now, all these years later, it appears that Nell has been searching for this same stepbrother—who is unquestionably a bad character—and every time she thinks she's close to him she happens to run into Mason Kirby. I don't think we're imagining things when we begin to suspect that Kirby had been chasing Lowry all these years. The present circumstances simply add to the presumption."

He faced Kirby for the first time. "You'll see my way of it, I hope, Mase. When I came home this afternoon, the subject was already under discussion. Nan knew as much about it as I did, of course. We'd talked about it many times, not out of idle curiosity, I assure you, but because we couldn't help but worry about the way a good friend's life had gotten so badly tangled. Anyway, Nan was afraid that Nell was getting involved in something that would become mighty painful for her, so she told her what I've just told you—or most of it. Now, do you want to give us your story?"

"I might as well," Kirby replied, trying to forget the expressions on the faces of the two women. "You've been exactly right on all of your guesses. Or maybe I shouldn't call them guesses. Just good thinking. You had only one advantage over me. I hadn't connected this Lowry visit with what had happened on the trail. I couldn't begin to put a name to any of the guilty parties, but I was sure they were guilty and I proposed to make them pay for their crime."

He laughed harshly and with no mirth whatever as he added, "I suppose I was pretty melodramatic about it—even if it was only to myself. I vowed to be the nemesis of the three men, even if it took me the rest of my life to run them down. It actually required nearly six months for me to get my first good lead. One of them had talked too much while he was drunk. I still had nothing that the law could use, but by that time I didn't intend to take the law into partnership with me. This was going to be a personal matter."

"You know better than that," Nan said reprovingly.

"Knowing and feeling are different things," he said shortly. "Anyway I had a name. Never mind what it was. The man is dead. But I didn't have the satisfaction of killing him. It's enough to tell you that I trailed him to the Montana gold camps and played the part of a miner while looking for him. I struck it rich, but I didn't find the man I wanted until after the Vigilantes had picked him up for a couple of other murders. Before they hanged him I persuaded him to tell me the

74

truth about what happened here. He named his companions. One of them was Joe Lowry."

"But how do you know it was Joe who did the actual killing?" Nell broke in, her voice almost hysterical.

"I don't. And it doesn't make a particle of difference. They were all equally guilty."

"Then you killed the second man?"

"No. I had much the same mixed luck that I'd had in Montana. I made a nice profit out of a trading trip to New Mexico, but the Apaches got number two before I did. I saw what they left and I was sick for a little while, but I wasn't sorry about any part of it except that I had again failed to carry out my objective. I came back from Montana just as I came back from New Mexico, richer but a bit depressed over failure. And all the more determined to make sure that Lowry didn't escape me."

"You don't even sound sane about it," Nell said wonderingly.

"Of course not. I haven't been sane on this subject at any time. Maybe that's why I'm able to talk about it so calmly now. Somehow this is something that isn't quite a part of me in spite of the fact that it's more important to me than anything else in the world. I've never let anything else interfere with carrying out the plans I made eight years ago."

He faced Nell directly. "Which brings me to

that other question you asked. I did not intend to use you to get at Joe Lowry. It was coincidence that I happened to run into you several times when both of us were hunting for him. After the first time I didn't want to see you again—but it happened."

"What do you mean you didn't want to see me again?"

"I had a feeling that you and I might have hit it off. We seemed to get along well together and we had a lot of things in common, including our personal tragedies. I liked you a lot and I thought you liked me. I couldn't afford to let myself fall in love with a woman whose stepbrother I proposed to kill."

She shuddered and looked away. He went on grimly, "You can see how it is. I wanted to spare you as much as I could. Then the tangle got worse here. What we proposed this afternoon would have been just a device to ease a different embarrassment until I could get away again."

"To murder Joe?" She stressed the word murder.

"You may call it that. Just as one of our troopers murdered a drunken Indian who had shot his lieutenant."

"That's hardly fair, Mase," Heilig protested. "I think there's a difference between retaliation in the heat of anger or danger and a grudge that has been nursed for eight years."

"So I'm not quite sane. That has already been said."

There was a long pause, no one wanting to say anything more when it seemed that too much had already been said. Finally it was Nell who tried once more. "Mason, were you sincere when you said that you were attracted to me but were afraid you might fall in love with me?"

"I was."

"Then I'll be completely frank with you. I was quite thrilled when I heard that you had come to Fort Fetterman. I had hopes that in our other meetings you might have come to like me. I would have been only too willing to marry you if you had asked me."

In spite of the grimness that had come upon him he could recognize what it had meant to her to make such a statement, particularly before the Heiligs.

"Thanks for trying," he told her. "But it's like I said a while ago. You and I might have made each other happy if there hadn't been this between us."

"But it doesn't have to be between us!" She was pleading now. "Forget this beastly vengeance. You're a civilized man, not a Sioux Indian!"

He shook his head. "Next to the day when they brought Mary's body in this is the worst day of my life." Then he left the room without another word.

There was still daylight enough for him to be

able to walk over toward the barracks, his mind struggling to find some clear program. Now he simply *had* to make that trip with the paymaster's party.

He kept clear of any part of the fort where he might run into officers, walking rapidly but aimlessly as he let the bitter thoughts race through his mind. Maybe they were right. Maybe he wasn't being quite sane about this. But when a man has spent eight years with one goal in mind, he isn't supposed to be quite normal on the subject.

Finally, when it was dark, he went back to his quarters, entering without speaking to anyone. For eight years he had cultivated a certain amount of sociability, making it part of the routine that was to keep him in some sort of emotional balance. He had done it knowingly, deliberately, just as he had gone out of his way to be cheerful with casual companions. Now he was in no mood to play games. The blackness was upon him, and it could stay there until he could get his hands on Joe Lowry.

It didn't. Presently he found himself thinking about Nell Perry. No matter how much he tried to avoid it, he thought about her and almost enjoyed it. The enjoyment had to be a sort of impersonal thing, of course. He had to remember her charm as something unreal, and he had to remember her declaration of affection as something to be appreciated but not really accepted. And he could admire the courage she had exhibited in doing what she must have considered to be quite unladylike. Then a sneaking little thought started to tell him that he was a fool to pass up a good life with Nell for a mere vengeance. He didn't even know that Joe Lowry had actually killed Mary.

That thought he would not accept. With an effort he forced his mind to the task of recalling details of the Fort Robinson area. Lowry must have a hideout there from which he had operated his whiskey-peddling business, a hideout which the military authorities had not been able to find. Maybe Mason Kirby could find it.

It was a long night, sleep coming only after hours of rolling and tossing with those bitter thoughts. He knew when reveille sounded but he did not get up, preferring to get some of the sleep he had missed and at the same time avoid having to meet Nell or the Heiligs. Having seen many paydays he was not very hopeful that Colonel Stanton would complete his duties at Fort Fetterman in time to move out toward Fort Robinson that afternoon. Since there would be a full day to kill, he preferred to kill it by himself.

The program worked out until after he had finally left his room long enough to eat a midday meal. Then there was an interruption. A Provost sergeant and two men came into the post trader's little dining room, accompanied by an embarrassed looking Sergeant Truitt.

"Is this the man, Sergeant?" The Provost non-com asked formally.

Truitt nodded. "That's him, all right." Then he bobbed his bullet head apologetically in Kirby's direction. "Sorry, Mistah Kuhby."

"Sorry for what?"

The Provost sergeant did the answering. "My orders are to place you under arrest, mister. Come along without any fuss, please." He was being very spruce and military about it, but he was also making it clear that he wasn't going to stand for any nonsense.

"What charge?" Kirby demanded.

"I don't know. I just have my orders. Come along please."

CHAPTER 6

The post guard house was not quite so formidable a structure as was the case in some of the older frontier forts Kirby had known. Like the rest of Fort Fetterman it was of frame construction, the walls looking flimsy enough so that any determined prisoner would have little trouble in breaking through. Still the windows were barred and the heavy door reinforced. There was one other inmate when Kirby found himself on the inside, his protests and demands to see an officer being completely ignored by the sergeant who had arrested him.

He was left in the single large room which made up a good two-thirds of the building, the balance being a row of narrow cells, one of which was now occupied by a tousled soldier with about three-days growth of reddish beard on his chin. Evidently the man was just beginning to get over the worst stages of a real roistering drunk.

"Ain't fair," the soldier told Kirby confidentially. "You'n me, we git loaded ahead o' payday and they t'row us in the pokey. T'night a hunnert men'll git drunk and nobody pays no 'tention. 'T'ain't fair!"

Kirby was in no mood to be entertained by a drunk. Outrage at the highhanded manner in which he had been arrested was now beginning to be mixed with a concern over what this would do to his chances of getting away with the paymaster's escort. Somebody was going to hear plenty about this! Arresting a civilian for no good cause on the strength of some silly emergency rules! At least he had to assume that emergency regulations must account for this illegal sort of arrest. And where was the guard officer? Why didn't somebody . . . ?

He forced himself into something a little more like ordinary anger, realizing that it wasn't doing a bit of good to rage around the calaboose for the entertainment of an inebriate. The soldier in the cell became comically sympathetic but could offer no information as to the routine of the guard house. He didn't know when the guard officer might come along. He didn't even know when the next meal would be served.

There was an enlisted man at the door, but he absolutely refused to say a word to either prisoner. The afternoon wore along and Kirby could hear the usual sounds of activity from the post, some of which he guessed might be Colonel Stanton actually making an afternoon departure. It was a little after five o'clock when a well tanned but still rosy cheeked lieutenant appeared at the guard house to ask courteously whether there might be anything he could do for the prisoner. The prisoner in this case meant Kirby.

The lieutenant was ignoring the man in the cell.

"Plenty you can do for me," Kirby stated wrathfully. "You can let me out of here. I'm a civilian and I'm not subject to army law. I've been arrested without a charge and detained without a hearing. Somebody's going to have a tough time explaining."

"Must be an oversight, Mr. Kirby," the lieutenant said soberly. "The charge was on file before you were arrested. Signed by Lieutenant Beckwith, I believe." The guard officer seemed almost cherubic in his concern. "I thought you had been informed."

"Nobody told me a thing!" Kirby snapped. "And who in hell is Lieutenant Beckwith?" Even as he asked the question he knew the answer. Beckwith was that paper work hound who had commanded the supply train's escort. And Sergeant Truitt had been with the arresting party. It was beginning to add up—but he didn't quite know how to explain the addition.

"I'm Lieutenant Cleophas," the guard officer told him courteously. It seemed as though being courteous was a part of the man. At least Kirby thought so and rather resented it. But then Kirby was in the mood to resent practically everything. "I'm on duty as guard officer but I don't mind telling you that the duty is quite distasteful to me. I don't . . ."

"I know. I've been a guard officer myself!"

"You were in the army?"

"I was." Kirby was getting grimmer by the moment. "But that's neither here nor there. I want to get out of here. I want to know what the charges are against me and I want counsel. Find Captain Heilig and tell him where I am. Report the matter to Major Hawkes. They'll do something."

Lieutenant Cleophas nodded solemnly. "You *are* disturbed, aren't you?" he murmured. "Very well, I'll do what I can."

When he was safely out of earshot, the drunk in the cell uttered one word. It wasn't a polite word, but it was obviously intended to express his low opinion of Lieutenant Cleophas. Kirby was inclined to agree.

Presently a guard brought food for both prisoners, remaining long enough to pass on a bit of gossip. He was clearly entertained at having a civilian in custody, but there was no malice in his attitude. "Kind of a dirty deal, I call it," he told Kirby. "You ain't done a thing the rest of us wouldn't ha' done. Ain't no call to git shoved in the pokey fer that."

"For what?" Kirby demanded. "Nobody has told me yet what I'm charged with doing."

"No. I figgered it was all over the post. They pulled you in fer killin' a Cheyenne. About a week ago, I hear tell."

Kirby was still fuming about the idiocy of the

charge when Lieutenant Cleophas returned with a sheaf of papers. "Got it all here," the cherub smile strongly in evidence. "I'll read you the important parts. Most of the rest of it is a lot of nonsense."

"It's all a lot of nonsense!"

"Probably. But here's how it goes. There's the usual order for the arrest of one Mason Kirby who, on the night of June sixteenth or the early morning of June seventeenth, eighteen hundred and seventy-six, did cause the death of a friendly Indian of the Cheyenne tribe, such tribe not being in insurrection against the United States but subject to its protection."

"Friendly Indian!" Kirby exclaimed. "The bastard tried to kill me in my sleep!"

"May I proceed? There is a rather lengthy indictment here."

"Skip the fancy words. What did Lieutenant Beckwith have to do with all this? He didn't know a thing about it."

The guard officer put away his papers almost reluctantly. Obviously he would have enjoyed reading the formal phrasings. "It's like this," he confided. "At inspection this morning a couple of troopers were found to have Indian property in their possession. They testified that they took the articles from a Cheyenne warrior who had been killed along the trail while they were acting as rear guards for the supply train which came up from Fort Laramie a few days ago. They further testified that you killed the Cheyenne. They also insisted that you had killed in self defense. Sergeant Truitt agreed with their testimony, but none of them had seen the actual killing. And it had never been reported to Lieutenant Beckwith who was the officer in charge out there. Naturally the lieutenant was annoyed at the breach of regulation and he insisted on a thorough investigation."

"The jackass! And who's doing any investigating? The only thing I seem to see happening is this business of keeping me in jail. I want somebody to represent me. Where's Captain Heilig and Major Hawkes?"

"Both of those officers have been with the commander all afternoon. I might tell you that there's a great deal of concern here about the orders regarding General Merritt's force on the South Cheyenne. General Sheridan has wired permission for the Fifth to be recalled."

"But they ought to . . ."

"Exactly. The area is quiet just now, but most of us believe that it will not remain quiet if the Fifth is recalled. And with the paymaster and his escort moving into that region it seems like a bad time to risk withdrawal of the force. Particularly when the paymaster permitted a lady to accompany him to Fort Robinson."

Kirby had to restrain himself with an effort. It

seemed as though this overly urbane guard officer was going out of his way to tell his story in the most aggravating manner possible. However, it would be no good to swear at him, no matter how great the temptation. Kirby wanted information, and, if he wanted to get it, then he had to restrain his impatience.

It took a lot of doing, but eventually the story came out so that it could be pieced together. Nell had indeed left Fort Fetterman for Fort Robinson, traveling with Colonel Stanton's escort under special permission from that official and from the post commander.

Kirby could guess why she had gone. What he couldn't understand was why she would take the risk when she must know now that the man she sought was a known criminal. His record was too clear for any argument about him.

"But what about this damned charge against me?" Kirby growled, getting back to the more important subject. "When do I get a chance to tell my story?"

Cleophas shrugged. "I'm just the guard officer. As an army man you know how little I have to say about such things. I'll do what I can."

"But it's pretty ridiculous."

"Some folks don't think so. We're living in a state of emergency. We have to keep the Indians peaceful down this way, if we can. Killing an Indian is not the way to do it."

"But the damned varmint tried to kill me!"

"You'll have to explain that at your trial. Like I said, I'm just the guard officer."

"Very well. But prod somebody, will you. I'm getting sorer by the minute."

A little later the place began to grow busy, the usual payday routine getting started. Payroll dollars were circulating with the normal celerity, arrests coming thick and fast as drunken brawls started in a dozen places. By ten o'clock the guard house was beginning to fill, a couple of fights breaking out inside the building as the prisoners were simply dumped into the big room. Kirby managed to keep reasonably clear of it by the simple expedient of moving into one of the unlocked cells and threatening to slug anyone who tried to open the door. Getting arrested was bad enough, but getting arrested on payday was a damned nuisance. Not to mention an outrage and a lot of other things.

It was nearly midnight when the Provost brought in three men who had missed Tattoo and had been found drunk in one of the cavalry stables. There was a flurry of cursing as the new arrivals were pushed in to stumble over other men sleeping it off on the hard floor. Then a lantern appeared and two voices rapped out commands for silence. One of the voices was that of Dutch Heilig.

In the muttering silence which followed Kirby

heard his name called. "Out here, Kirby," Heilig ordered.

Kirby stepped gingerly over the sprawled figures on the jail floor and presently was standing in the light of the lantern just outside the guard house door. Captain Heilig and Lieutenant Cleophas were awaiting him, wry grins apparent on both sets of features. He resented the grins enough to snap, "Maybe I should have stayed in there. The company was better."

Heilig still grinned as he retorted. "Go on back then. It's your choice. But I thought you wanted to get out."

"Aw, shut up! What kind of damned fool business is brewing now?"

"Come along. We'll talk later." As he swung away he spoke over his shoulder to the lieutenant. "Nine o'clock sharp, Lieutenant. And remember your orders."

Then they were moving across through the darkness, the lantern having been left with the guard officer. Kirby waited until they had almost reached the post trader's establishment, but then he asked, "What's my status now?"

"You're still under arrest. I thought you'd prefer to sleep in your own quarters."

"Under guard?"

"We'll have a sentry outside. You're still under arrest, remember."

"When do I get a hearing?"

"I'm working on it."

Further questions brought no satisfaction at all and in a matter of minutes Kirby was left to himself, still as angry as ever but at least alone.

No one came near him again until Hank Weightman brought him breakfast fairly late in the morning. The post trader was inclined to be amused by the whole affair and his greeting hinted at the mood.

"Thought you wouldn't be in no hurry, Kirby. After a big night in the tank with the drunks I thought mebbe you'd want to get yourself some sleep."

"Save the jokes," Kirby growled. "From my side it's not funny."

"I reckon not. To me there's somethin' real humorous about it. A lot o' my customers have gone from here to the jug but I figure it's the first time I ever had one come from the jug to here."

"Got any idea how long they plan to go on with this farce?"

Weightman shrugged. "Hard to tell. Officers have got a lot on their minds today. Merritt's ordered out o' the Cheyenne basin—and just when it looks like the Injuns might be stirrin'."

"I thought things were quiet."

"Can't tell. We finally got some o' the Rosebud yarn. Seems like General Crook wasn't altogether truthful with his report. His outfit took somewhat of a beatin' in the fight and they mighta got it a lot worse if'n some o' the Cheyennes hadn't made an attack at the wrong time."

"Go on. What's the yarn?"

"Well, it seems as though Crazy Horse had a real nice trap all set fer one o' the columns that was aimin' to attack the Injun village. They was almost in the nutcracker when these here Cheyennes started an attack at another part of the line and Crook ordered his attack column back to support the middle of the line. They'd ha' been wiped out if it hadn't happened that way."

"I see. Then he had to use his whole force to prevent a real defeat?"

"Seems that way. The Injuns didn't pull back until they started brawlin' among themselves over the way the Cheyenne attack spoiled the big strategy. Anyway that's how the scouts figure it happened."

"I wonder how the Indians at the Agency will interpret it?"

"That's what worries everybody. From here it looks like they won the fight. It could be just enough to stir 'em up."

"Or it could be that the Cheyennes will feel that they are in disgrace. Maybe other Cheyennes won't be so anxious to join the Sioux while they're under a sort of tribal stigma."

"Go ahead and guess," Weightman invited. "Everybody else is doin' it."

"Any news from the other armies?"

"Same as it was. They're movin' in. Funny thing about it is that we're more up-to-date on Terry and Gibbon than we are on Crook. Mostly it's a good three days before we get a message through from Crook, but the telegraph brings us the story of what them other fellers are doing in a little over a day. Great world we're livin' in these days."

"Yeah, great." Kirby didn't try to hide his sarcasm. A man whose personal troubles were almost as complicated as the highly inflammable Indian situation couldn't be expected to enthuse very much over a telegraph system that could send messages back and forth across the country in such remarkable time. Actually it wasn't all the telegraph, he realized, even though he kept telling himself that he was not interested. Terry's communications back to the nearest wire station had to be mighty good. After that it was mechanical.

It was just nine o'clock when he had visitors. Major Hawkes, Captain Heilig, and Lieutenant Cleophas filed in solemnly, offering formal greetings and disposing themselves as comfortably as possible in the little room. Hawkes took the room's only chair, motioning for Kirby to seat himself between the other two officers on the bed. Then he pulled a sheaf of papers from an inner pocket and announced, "I declare this emergency court martial in session. Major

William Hawkes presiding, Lieutenant Cleophas in charge of the prisoner and also appearing for Lieutenant Beckwith who preferred charges but is not present in court. Captain Heilig acts as counsel for the accused. Accused also waives formal indictment in view of conditions now pertaining at this post."

He dropped his formal air to inquire of Kirby, "No objection."

It was Heilig who replied, giving Kirby a quick elbow. "No objections, sir."

Hawkes then proceeded to cover in some detail—and with something of a flourish—what Cleophas had already told Kirby. Then he added, "On behalf of the accused there has been submitted affidavits of Sergeant Truitt and Privates Bradway, Collins, and Ernst to the effect that the Cheyenne killed by Mr. Kirby had previously discharged an arrow into a dummy which he clearly believed to be this same Kirby. All four of these men believe that the Cheyenne was killed in self defense after an unprovoked attack upon what he must have believed to be a sleeping man. Lieutenant Cleophas, have you anything to say for the prosecution?"

"No, sir. The statement covers all that pertains to the accused."

"Captain Heilig?"

"The defense statement is substantially that of the enlisted men, sir?"

"Mr. Kirby?"

"That's exactly how it was and I want to protest . . ."

"The court finds the accused not guilty. He is hereby discharged from custody with the apologies of the court for the inconvenience caused him. Court is dismissed."

He dropped the formal tone to add, "Sorry about all this, Kirby. I'm afraid Lieutenant Beckwith is something of a stickler for regulations. He was a bit outraged that the matter had not been properly reported."

"Any trouble for the men, sir?"

Hawkes grinned, the expression oddly at variations with his usual show of pompous dignity. "Lieutenant Beckwith is now on his way back to Fort Laramie with a train of empty wagons. The report will show that this court was held and that the enlisted men in question were sentenced to extra duty for failure to make a proper report. I believe Captain Heilig saw to that matter."

He was on his way out of the room when Heilig murmured, "Sergeant Truitt and his men were put on special assignment as guards for a lady who is traveling to Fort Robinson with Colonel Stanton's escort. I hope that'll satisfy Beckwith."

"It won't satisfy me," Kirby warned him grimly. "This whole deal stinks. I want to know who's trying to do what."

CHAPTER 7

Heilig moved across to the chair before replying. Then he seemed to pull himself together as though preparing for a distasteful chore. "I'll tell you the whole truth, Mase, and hope you won't hold it against me."

"Then you cooked up this trick to detain me?"

"No. It really happened the way you just heard. But I could have done something about it much sooner. Major Hawkes is a pretty good fellow, as you may recognize by this time. He'd have listened if I had gone to him and made an immediate protest. I didn't do it. On that score I'm guilty of causing you to be held up. I imagine you know why."

"Trying to protect me from myself, I suppose you'd call it."

"Don't sound so bitter. I had a choice to make. Nell heard about Stanton's projected move and asked me to do what I could to see that she could go along with him. I had a simple but not easy choice. I could let either or both of you head for Fort Robinson. I decided that it would be better for Nell to go. Again you must understand why."

"So that damned Lowry can sneak away without getting what's coming to him!"

"Mase, I don't give one little thin damn about

Joe Lowry. He's a thug of the worst sort, I'm sure, but I'd rather let him get clear than to have you go through with this crazy vengeance scheme of yours. In the long run it would hurt you far more than killing would hurt him. I honestly believe that."

"Is that what Nell claimed as her motive also?"

"No. She wanted to reach him before you could find him, hoping that she could get him to give himself up and stand trial."

"Don't tell me you consider that sensible!"

"Frankly I don't. But Nell believed it would work. I think she would have tried almost anything to keep you from getting your hands bloody on him. You're pretty much of a fool, Mase."

"Thanks. For everything, including the kind words."

"I mean it. If you kill Joe Lowry, it'll be between you and Nell for all time. If you let him go—or let the authorities have him for some of his more recent crimes—you might find that you and Nell could work something out together. And I believe that's exactly what she has in mind."

"That makes me a fool?"

"You're damned right it does. If a woman like Nell Perry was making bright eyes at me—and I didn't happen to be married to Nan—I'd think twice before I'd pass her up for petty vengeance."

Kirby shook his head. "I'm not asking for logic. This is something I'm bound to do. Give my best to Nan. I'll be leaving here just as soon as I can get ready."

Heilig stood up. "I won't wish you luck, Mase. Not on this. But take care of yourself. That country over around the Agency could get hotter than a Sioux torture fire at any moment."

He offered his hand and Kirby took it, squeezing firmly for just a moment. Then Heilig went out and Kirby started to pack his scanty belongings. Colonel Stanton's party had less than twenty-four hours start. Maybe he could still reach Fort Robinson ahead of a party that would be limited to the speed of the clumsy ambulances. It would probably take the paymaster's party three days to make the journey. Kirby figured he could do it in less than two.

When he had stuffed extra garments into saddlebags he went out to find Weightman. The post trader's charge for the lodging was modest enough, and Kirby congratulated himself that he was again in the odd position of having made a profit out of a trip which was not supposed to be a profit-making affair. Of course he would have to wait for his share of the whiskey deal, but he felt sure that his temporary partner would be good for it.

"My horse and gear in your stable?" he asked. "Major Hawkes was to have everything brought over here after I sold the wagon outfit."

"I've got the horse, all right," Weightman told

him. "Stable bill was included in what I just listed there. But I don't remember any saddle or other gear."

A search of the stable showed nothing. The liveryman who worked for Weightman didn't appear to be very bright, but he was positive about the matter of Kirby's horse. The animal had been brought to him by a farrier corporal named McCann. There hadn't even been a bridle on the horse at the time.

Kirby swore under his breath and went in search of Captain Heilig. The only way to run down a lost saddle in a place like Fort Fetterman was to do it through regular channels. Anyway the army had lost it; let the army have the job of finding it.

The thought didn't help to ease his impatience. Time was moving along—and Colonel Stanton's party was doing the same thing. Every hour of delay made his chances of beating the escort to Fort Robinson all the more slim.

It took him the better part of an hour to find Heilig. Then he took a note to a sergeant who was in charge of the post stables. The sergeant was decent enough about it, but he didn't know anything about an extra saddle and he had never heard of a Corporal McCann. With the garrison having had so many recent changes in personnel that was not surprising. There was a good chance that the corporal in question might now be on his way to join Crook or perhaps even in Stanton's escort. One way or another there was no trace of the saddle.

By that time the afternoon was almost gone and Kirby went back to Heilig. Again the wheels of procedure began to turn but Kirby didn't wait; he proceeded to search the post for some civilian who might have a saddle to sell. When he took time out for a late supper, he knew that there was not an extra saddle on the post. A half hour later he was informed that no amount of tracing or searching had produced the missing one. By that time he was willing to call the whole thing off. The chance of overtaking Stanton's party was already gone.

He moved back into the same room he had occupied, spending the evening in dour silence and refusing to let Heilig in when the captain came along to report continued failure.

"I've done everything I could, Mase," Heilig called softly through the closed door. "But I won't try to tell you that I'm sorry I failed. I've got a pretty good idea of what you were planning to do."

"Go to hell!" Kirby growled.

"In my own way. I'm glad it isn't the way you're so damned set on taking."

Then he went away and Kirby had another sleepless night. Part of the time he lay awake cursing the army and everyone in it. Then he cursed himself for being such a fool. Then he thought about Nell Perry and cursed himself even more. By dawn he was almost convinced that he might as well give up on Joe Lowry and try to get back to something like normalcy. These past few days were turning him into the sort of semi-madman that he had always promised himself he would not become.

Exhaustion finally claimed him and when he awoke it was mid-morning. Now he didn't care. His margin of time was gone. There was no longer any point in trying to reach Fort Robinson or the Red Cloud Agency. He decided that his best move was to wait for the next train of empty wagons going down to Fort Laramie. He could travel on a wagon and simply get away from the whole damned country. Somehow it didn't much matter whether he ever found Joe Lowry.

He kept clear of the officers he had come to know, learning from stable gossip that there were no more wagons scheduled to leave. Probably the next wagon train would be the one coming down from the north with the wounded from the Rosebud fight and no one knew just when they might be expected to arrive. Kirby went back to his room again and slept through the heat of a stifling afternoon. After the tension and the anger he felt spent, reaction affecting him physically as well as emotionally.

On the following day he was almost as

lethargic, rousing long enough to discuss various items of information that had come in. General Merritt was on his way to Fort Laramie. The South Cheyenne patrol was called off, General Sheridan being of the opinion that it had served its purpose and that the Indians at the Red Cloud Agency would cause no trouble. General Crook was preparing a new advance and had done some extensive scouting without finding Sioux in any strength. It was believed that the delaying action fought by Crazy Horse on the Rosebud had been only a token resistance and that the hostiles had fled northward, probably right into the teeth of those other armies.

The accounts could be interpreted in a number of ways, but the general feeling was one of optimism. The Indians weren't really anxious to fight. When they found themselves surrounded, they would permit themselves to be herded back to their reservations. The campaign was about over.

It was late in the afternoon that the telegraph began to crackle a story which silenced the optimists. General Terry's advance detachment had run into some sort of trouble. At first the information was fragmentary and a little tangled. Men who understood the way such information must have been received had to hope that confusion could account for the darker picture others were seeing. They knew that a field report from

Terry's headquarters would have gone back by messenger to where it could be put on a wire to St. Louis. At that point an operator had relayed it to General Sheridan at Fort Laramie. Fetterman was getting only a sort of telegraph rumor. There had been an action of some sort, they knew, but the general belief was that it wasn't so bad as the story made it sound.

"It could be bad enough," Heilig told Kirby soberly. "Custer had the advance and you know what that would mean. If he found the hostiles he'd try to hit them just as hard as he could."

"And at the wrong time."

"What do you mean by that?"

Kirby chuckled—for the first time in days. "You keep forgetting our formula for Indian war. The first battles are the worst for our side. Crook almost got caught in an ambush, so it's pretty likely that the Sioux would have tried the same game on the other columns. Custer might be just the fellow to smash right into such an ambush. And while the Indians are still at fighting peak."

"Gloomy character, aren't you."

"About Indians—yes. I still think we had it figured just about right. Even lieutenants can be correct once in a while."

"It isn't often," Heilig retorted. "But I'll give you a chance to see if a captain can guess right. I'll buy you a new saddle—the first time we can find one—if Sheridan doesn't order the Fifth to stay on their patrol station. This could be the news that might set the Agency Indians on the warpath."

"Merritt's already coming in, I understand."

"So I understand. I'll bet there's a messenger on his way to meet them at this very moment, ordering them back on patrol. It's vital."

On the following morning Kirby checked with his best source of gossip, Hank Weightman, and learned that the Fifth was still supposed to be heading for Fort Laramie. There had been no further details on what had happened up there north of the Powder, and the official statement was that everything was going according to plan. Merritt would halt patrol activities and come back to the Platte. Kirby promptly called on Captain Heilig and asked for a saddle.

Heilig gave him a wry smile and led the way outside. Behind his office a saddle hung across a hitch rack. Kirby stared at it and exclaimed, "Mine! Don't tell me you kept on playing tricks and hid it!"

"I'd feel hurt by that accusation if I didn't feel that you have good grounds to suspect me. Actually it was found under some hay in the stables. My private opinion is that one of our sterling troopers stole it and hid it there. I even think I know who the man was. Under the circumstances I'm not going to voice those suspicions. I think the thief did you a favor."

"Maybe. But I'm entitled to a new saddle, not this old one."

Heilig shrugged. "Some people are never satisfied. So I owe you a saddle. Maybe I'll find a cheap one somewhere."

Kirby laughed. It felt good. He hadn't laughed for quite a while. "Funny I can laugh at a bum joke like that. I'm sure there's nothing funny about the way this mess is shaping up."

"Good sign," Heilig told him. "You don't sound half as much like the messenger of doom as you did the other night. But what don't you like about the current picture."

"I don't like any of it. I think Merritt ought to stay on the South Cheyenne."

"Especially now."

"Especially now. Very well. I'm thinking about Nell being over there, but I'm also thinking of the general conditions. Until we know what happened to Terry's advance detachment, I don't think we ought to let up one little bit on our control of the South Cheyenne."

Heilig nodded soberly. "All of that *we* stuff makes it sound as though you'd taken the army into partnership with you again. Maybe that's good. I told you the other day that we were mighty short of scouts who know the country to the east. Right now you're the only man in the place who has ever been a dozen miles east of the North Platte canyon. In an emergency you might turn out to be real handy."

"Now you want to send me to Fort Robinson! For the past few days you've been playing all kinds of sneaky tricks to keep me from going there. What's the idea?"

"Nell's there now. I think she can handle you, mister!"

Kirby grimaced but didn't reply. Mostly because he didn't know whether to be annoyed, sheepish, or even a little pleased. Next time—if there should be a next time—he didn't think an old grudge would stand in the way of his coming to some sort of understanding with Nell. Joe Lowry just wasn't so important any longer.

In mid-afternoon the telegraph became active once more and this time details began to come through. Even allowing for the way in which the message had been relayed, it was fairly clear that there had been a major disaster somewhat to the north of the spot where General Crook had been stopped by Crazy Horse. The Seventh Cavalry, led by General Custer, had moved out ahead of Terry's main force and had found the main concentration of Sioux as ordered. Then—but not as ordered—they had attacked a large village on the Little Bighorn, known to the Sioux as the Greasy Grass. A large part of the Seventh had been wiped out, and Custer himself had been killed.

Further messages added to the gloomy story.

Custer had not only attacked in direct disobedience of Terry's orders, but he had divided his regiment in the face of that immense force of Sioux and Cheyennes. His personal detachment had been completely exterminated, and the other two units had been mauled quite badly before forting up on a hill and standing siege until Gibbons men rescued them.

By nightfall enough of it was clear for men to be gravely concerned. Unquestionably the Sioux had scored a great victory. Actually the number of men killed in the battle would not be more than about 300, thus making it relatively small in terms of military history, but for the Sioux it would have immense moral value. For the Cheyennes it would be even more significant. It had been Cheyennes who had suffered from Custer's tactics on the Washita; his death would fan a real spark with that particular tribe.

"I think I'll get ready to ride," Kirby told Heilig in a grim voice. "General Sheridan must know what this will mean to the Custer-hating Cheyennes. That mixture of Cheyennes and Sioux at Fort Robinson will bust wide open. He's got to order Merritt back on patrol!"

"Could be," Heilig agreed. "But don't get too anxious. We don't know how far Merritt may have marched toward Fort Laramie. They may send a scout from there, if they have one. The last time I heard any talk about it they were as bad off for scouts as we were. Merritt took every available man when he left for the South Cheyenne, even though General Carr had organized a big scout company when he still had the regiment."

Kirby nodded thoughtfully. "On such a job he'd need plenty of scouts. You don't happen to know whether he had old Joe Brucker or Thad McManus, do you? They knew the South Cheyenne better than most men."

"That was the trouble. Along with the troops from the Third who did patrol work there last year every scout worth his salt went with General Crook. Brucker and McManus weren't available when Carr took the Fifth on patrol. As a matter of fact Carr brought in some of his own scouts, including this Bill Cody who has been touring the eastern states with a Wild West Show. Merritt has some good men with him, but they're not too familiar with this bit of country."

They were interrupted then as Major Hawkes came in, his face stern. "Mr. Kirby, are you willing to undertake a job for us? After all the trouble we've made for you?"

Kirby nodded, a small grin showing as it occurred to him that the adjutant was a man of many moods. At first he had seemed overly pompous. Then he had displayed a dry sort of humor. Now he was worried, almost humble. "Captain Heilig and I were just talking about it.

I assume that you mean a job connected with getting a message to General Merritt."

"And you're willing?"

"Of course."

"We don't have orders yet but Laramie has been asking us about it. They don't have anyone who knows the country, and it appears that the commanding general is preparing new orders."

"I'll be ready." He aimed a wry grimace at Heilig as he added, "Now that I have a saddle once more I think I can make it."

Hawkes bustled out and Kirby went immediately to make sure that his horse was in proper condition and to prepare his gear. Heilig issued orders for hard rations and an extra canteen, the whole business of getting ready not requiring more than ten minutes. Then they sat down to wait.

By midnight both men had lost their enthusiasm. The army was playing the drear old game of "hurry up and wait." No further word had come from Fort Laramie except for additional details on the Custer debacle. Five full companies of the Seventh had been cleaned out, no survivor left to tell exactly what had happened. The detachment commanded by Major Reno had also suffered severe casualties. Major Benteen's unit had provided the reserve which saved Reno, the two groups taking further mauling during the two-day siege which followed. Gibbon's column had apparently scattered the victorious hostiles, but it was not yet known which direction the Indians had taken. They might even have evaded Crook and headed south toward the Platte or the South Cheyenne.

There was still no order next morning and again the weary, tense business of waiting put everyone on edge. A messenger came in from Crook but he had heard nothing of the Custer fight, even though it was now known that the Little Bighorn massacre had occurred only scant miles away from the Rosebud battlefield. In spite of telegraph lines the Indian communications seemed to be far superior to those of their white enemies.

The day dragged on, everyone irritable and worried. Finally, with the afternoon almost spent, an orderly summoned Kirby to headquarters. This time Colonel Mears, commandant of the post, was with Adjutant Hawkes. There were no preliminaries beyond the briefest of introductions. Hawkes took over the meeting.

"We have an order for General Merritt, Mr. Kirby. You are still willing to undertake the task of finding him?"

"That was the agreement."

"There's a complication. Our information is not clear as to when he expected to start his march toward Fort Laramie, so we don't have any idea as to his present location. Do you think you can find him?"

Kirby pointed to a rough map on the wall. He could see at a glance that it was sadly lacking in detail but it would serve his purpose. He used a ruler from the adjutant's desk to point out a spot immediately south of the Black Hills. "General Merritt should have had his patrol headquarters near this spot. It would have permitted him to control the major trails north from the Agency. A march to Fort Laramie from that spot would have involved a sort of detour to the west and then southwest. It's the best way to avoid the rugged country along a number of creeks which don't show here. With wagons he would have had to avoid the direct route. I propose to strike for this point." He indicated another bare patch about halfway between the South Cheyenne and Fort Laramie. "If General Merritt has not already passed the place I'll be pretty sure that he's somewhere to the northeast and coming toward me."

"And if he has passed it?"

"I'll see the tracks and know that it'll be too late for me to catch him before he reaches Laramie."

"Very well. You know better than we do. You're ready to ride?"

"I've been ready for twenty-four hours."

"Fine. I'm putting you on the rolls as a civilian scout."

"Don't do it. I prefer to be a volunteer. When the message is delivered, I'll be on my own. That's the way I want it."

He knew that Hawkes understood something of the situation, and he could see the brief shadow which passed across the major's face. There was no argument, however. The adjutant simply handed him a paper, folded but not sealed.

"General Sheridan's orders are for General Merritt to bring the Fifth directly to Fort Fetterman instead of continuing to Fort Laramie. From this point they will march without delay to join General Cook."

Kirby stared. "You mean the South Cheyenne is to be left unguarded?"

"That's the way it is." Both Hawkes and Mears were trying to look stolid, but there was no doubt as to their feelings. Both were aghast at this change in orders. General Sheridan had been getting some mighty bad advice.

"You're still willing to undertake the mission?" Colonel Mears asked.

"I'll go. General Merritt should know what has happened. And the Agency should be informed."

They shook hands quickly and Kirby went out. This wasn't exactly what he had bargained for, but in the army there could be no second guessing of the commander. Maybe General Crook would need Merritt's help a lot more than the Agency would. At least that was one way of looking at it.

CHAPTER 8

Heilig was waiting when Kirby came out of the headquarters building. "When do you start?" he asked bluntly.

"After dark. Now that it's so late a couple of hours won't make much difference and it may be safer that way. Those Indians camped outside the post may be peaceful and they may not be. If I leave after dark, there won't be so much chance that I'll be having somebody on my trail."

"Sounds smart. I had your horse taken across on the ferry when you first went in to see the commander. You'll be leaving from the other side, I presume?"

Kirby nodded. "Smart move, Dutch. I'll get a man to row me across so it won't look like anything important going on. You stay on this side. Then they won't see any move that involves an officer."

"Right. One thing, Mase. You're not going to let your other interest interfere, are you?"

"It won't interfere. I'll still get Lowry if it's humanly possible, but I don't propose to even think about him until I've found the Fifth and delivered this message."

"Then?"

"You can guess. If Nell hasn't scared him off

I still might have a chance at him. I've been looking for that sonofabitch for eight years and I don't think I'll get too sentimental about him now!"

Again Heilig offered his hand. "I can't wish you luck on that part, Mase. As I said before, just take care of yourself—and don't forget how Nell must feel."

Ten minutes later he crossed the Platte in a small boat rowed by two enlisted men, the crossing purposely slow and casual. If any of the Indians camped along the river were watching the fort for the hostiles they would have seen nothing that wasn't happening almost hourly. The traffic across to the outpost stables was a routine matter, and Kirby made certain that he moved into the routine. Since his horse and gear were already across, he didn't even have to carry anything with him.

With almost two hours of daylight left he took his time, not even approaching the stables until several minutes after making the crossing. Then he found a pile of clean hay and went to sleep, summoning the old knack as a means of building up his staying power for the long ride ahead. He might have as much as a hundred miles to go before he could complete his errand, and he didn't want to start off tired.

Somehow he found himself quite relaxed. The job ahead would be tough and dangerous, but he didn't feel either excitement or tension. The waiting was over, along with the uncertainty. Now he knew what he had to do—and he had a pretty good idea of what he might also be able to do.

When he awakened he found that dusk was already settling across the Platte valley, a hot dusk which might presage thunderstorms during the night. The idea didn't bother him too much. His first hours in the saddle would be over completely familiar ground and a bit of a storm might help to keep him clear of spying eyes.

He was just getting out of the hay when a farrier sergeant came in to awaken him. "Wish I could sleep like that, mister," the sergeant told him. "We got grub waitin'. Better fill up while you're waitin' fer full dark. No tellin' when you'll get your next meal."

Kirby knew that there would be no moonrise until shortly after ten o'clock, so he would have several hours of darkness for his purpose, perhaps even more if a storm developed. He went with the sergeant, swallowed a hot meal, and hurried on across to the stables where his horse was ready and waiting, saddlebags in place and cinches tight. It was a matter of seconds for him to be in the saddle and moving along the river bank. No watchful eye must realize that he was going somewhere in a hurry.

He was a good mile east of the last tepees when

he urged the pony to a faster pace. Sheridan's pace, they had called it back in the Shenandoah and later on the frontier. Alternate walking and trotting. It kept horses fresher and ate up the miles. He tried to remember the terrain so as to risk the trot on level ground and keep to a walking pace where the ground was more uneven.

An hour after leaving the stables he cut away from the bend of the river, taking a more easterly course as the Platte swung to the south. He could only hope now that he had called the turn correctly in the colonel's office. A large command such as Merritt's would have a considerable baggage train. So they would have to come up the South Cheyenne as far as Saco Creek to avoid the broken country along those headwater creeks of the Niobrara. Then they could follow Rawhide Creek until reaching open country where they could strike directly for Fort Laramie. He wanted to catch them before they left Rawhide. Otherwise they'd reach Laramie before he could find them. Unless he cut them off they would waste hours and miles in reaching the more southerly post only to turn north and march extra miles to get back to Fort Fetterman. It might make a difference of several days in the time needed to reinforce General Crook. And Crook might now stand between the victorious hostiles and the Platte. Nobody could be sure just now.

For the better part of an hour lightning flared viciously in the north and he could catch glimpses of the sullen clouds piled up in that direction, but the thunder was a low rumble and he concluded that he was riding parallel to the storm, just off the southern fringes of it. Once he rode through a light sprinkle of rain, but then the disturbance died away and the night around him was calm.

Then the rising moon made a fine beacon in the east and he made good time in its light. By midnight it had climbed high enough so that he was able to find his way through the dry washes and gullies, not quite sure whether these would be tributaries—in the rainy season—of the Cheyenne or the Platte. Not that it made much difference as long as they were small and dry. While he found nothing resembling a real stream he knew that he was following the divide between the two rivers, the same divide which Merritt's column would have to follow before they could turn south toward Fort Laramie.

The night travel actually seemed pleasant, only an occasional whiff of alkali on the breeze reminding him of what this arid country was like in the heat of day. At midnight he rested his horse for twenty minutes and then went on at a cautious pace, walking once in a while to stretch his legs as well as to save the pony's strength. He knew that he had a good mount, but he wasn't in any mood to take chances. No more than were necessary, that is. This country might be swarming with a fresh batch of hostiles and he didn't propose to find himself in open country with an exhausted horse.

At the first break of dawn he rested again, waiting for daylight this time so that he could take a good look at the surrounding terrain before making his next move. He didn't believe that he could be far off the course he had set for himself, but he wanted to play it as safe as possible. Sunrise showed him a barren land of yellows and browns, a few buttes to the north and some rolling country to the south. Nowhere was there a column of smoke or a trail of dust. The way was clear.

He moved on at the same dogged pace, angling just a little more to the north as he became more confident that Merritt's force had not yet left the divide. They might have cut at a sharper angle, but he didn't think it would have happened that way. They had been in the country long enough for veteran scouts to have learned that much about it. Wagons wouldn't use any such shortcut unless they went around by way of the Agency and then west.

Within the hour the morning sun began to beat at him, but he kept to the mile-eating pace, pausing for regular rest stops and occasionally to climb a butte for observation. By noon he could make out the line of cottonwoods which he knew would mark the headwaters of some obscure fork of the Niobrara. The land was rocky, cut by deep gullies, and completely unsuitable for wagon travel. Merritt's column certainly hadn't tried to use this region.

Again he shifted to a more northerly angle. If Merritt had played it safe, taking a really long angle of march there was just a chance that Kirby might overreach himself and let the Fifth swing in behind him. That blunder he had to avoid.

Almost at once he began to hit smoother country, and flashes of memory told him that he was doing all right. This was the proper line of march for a command with baggage. Merritt ought to be using it. And he definitely had not come through here as yet. There wasn't any sign at all.

Shortly before noon he spotted a tiny trailer of dust in the southeast, so he halted promptly, taking shelter behind a low bluff which rose out of the otherwise flat mesquite barrens. From its crest he studied the distant figures which he could see beneath the dust, coming to the conclusion that he was looking at a small band of Indians, probably not more than six or eight. What was more important to him was that they were moving away into the southeast. With his present path leading northeast they shouldn't represent any threat.

Then he had a hunch. Probably this was a

gang of restless young bucks from the Agency who had been keeping an eye on Merritt's force. Now they were headed for home, possibly to pass the word that the cavalry were actually leaving the South Cheyenne. In one sense it was a cheerful interpretation because it meant that the Fifth would be not many miles ahead, probably marching up Saco Creek before making the break south toward Fort Laramie. But there was a less cheering aspect. If the Indians had been watching Merritt, it meant that they were still plenty interested in him. Perhaps they were only waiting for his departure before making some kind of hostile move. Kirby could only hope that Merritt had left some sort of detachment at the Red Cloud Agency to keep a keen watch on the Indians. Things were bad enough without having these southern Sioux and Cheyennes break loose to join Sitting Bull.

He moved on again at a brisker pace, risking the stamina of his horse on the hunch that his journey was almost at an end. And it didn't seem likely that he would have to fear any Indian attack upon himself. Even if those distant warriors noticed his dust they probably had more on their minds than a chase after a single unknown rider.

Less than an hour later he saw the dust against the sky ahead. There was a lot of it, so he decided that he was about to meet the marching Fifth Cavalry. Still he played it safe, remembering that there was still a risk that the northern hostiles might have struck south after their victory over Custer. He slowed the pace, avoiding dust as much as possible and finally halting behind another of those chalky yellow outcroppings which dotted the land. As an old hand at Indian warfare he didn't propose to make elementary mistakes. It took patience, but finally he could make out the advance riders. They wore blue. It was mighty dusty blue, but he was satisfied. The Fifth was indeed proceeding up Saco Creek, preparatory to the swing southward that he had anticipated. It brought him a quick satisfaction that he had figured it out correctly, but then he was moving again, aware that he had been spotted and that some of the advance guard was coming forward to have a look at him.

Ten minutes later he delivered his dispatches to the red-faced and sweating General Merritt, adding his own observations on the subject of those warriors he had seen riding toward the Agency.

Somewhat to his chagrin no one wanted to pay any attention to that extra bit of information. The story of the Custer disaster seemed to leave them all a bit numb and for some time the column remained where it had halted, no orders being issued to march, fall out, or anything else. Officers who had had friends in the Seventh seemed to have suffered body blows. Talk was almost in whispers except when an oath would burst forth. Kirby understood. He had seen the same kind of reaction at Fort Fetterman—and there the news had not come in one stunning dose.

It was General Merritt himself who seemed to recover first. "We'll make camp here while we still have water," he told his adjutant. "All company commanders meet me here in half an hour. Lieutenant King, will you see to it that information goes back to Lieutenant Hall at the wagon train?"

Almost as an afterthought he added, "Captain Hyde, attend to this man and see that both he and his horse get the best possible attention. Bring him with you to the meeting."

The wagons began to come up while Kirby was eating the rations set out for him. Instantly he became alert. There were extra men on every wagon and others walked along beside them. Civilians and not necessarily teamsters. Maybe Joe Lowry would be in this group. If the man wanted to get away from the charges the army wanted to press against him, he might well have slipped into these disorderly ranks.

Kirby commented casually to a corporal who had come along to hear the story of the Custer defeat. "Seems like you've got a lot of teamsters with this outfit."

The man shook his head, shooting out a stream

of tobacco juice before making an oral reply. "Extra men. Not teamsters. For a month we've been pickin' up such gold hunters as managed to get past the Injuns. We had a hell of a time workin' the patrols both ways, tryin' to keep the Injuns from goin' into the Black Hills and tryin' to rescue the damned fools that didn't get out before some of the Injuns got in."

Kirby hadn't thought about that part. He had heard of Merritt's duty as being only the problem of keeping the reservation Indians from joining the hostiles. Now he realized that it had been a lot more complicated than that. "Lots of refugee miners in Cheyenne and Fort Laramie," he commented. "It's hard to believe there were so many of them working this territory."

"There was more," the corporal told him dryly. "A whole passel didn't git out."

"You didn't happen to run into one of them by the name of Joe Lowry, did you?" He thought he might as well ask it that way. If Joe was with the regiment he would probably be masquerading as a miner.

"Ain't heard no names at all," the corporal retorted. "Just men."

Kirby altered his own plans immediately. He had intended to get away as quickly as possible and head for the Red Cloud Agency, but now he knew that he might be missing a good bet. He had to remain with the Fifth until he could find time to look over this crowd of miners. And he didn't actually know Joe Lowry by sight. A memorized description would have to do; there shouldn't be too many men in this outfit who weighed around a hundred and seventy pounds, stood five feet ten and had a couple of upper teeth missing in front.

He started to make his canvas immediately, but a messenger from Captain Hyde caught up with him before he had seen twenty men. General Merritt's council-of-war was about to go into session.

It caught him completely by surprise when he heard his name called just as he moved into the group which was finding seats around the commander's ambulance. "Mase Kirby! So it was you who brought that message about the Seventh! I thought you left the army years ago!"

Kirby stared, then grinned and took the hand which was being thrust toward him. "Jim Gibson! I didn't know you at first with all that alfalfa on your face. Somehow you're prettier that way."

There was a nervous chuckle from the other officers and then Kirby resumed, "I brought the message all right but only as a civilian volunteer. I resigned my commission eight years ago." He was thinking that the eight years had done a lot to Gibson. It had put an extra bar on his shoulders, but it had given him a lot of unhealthy weight around the belt line and a crop of wrinkles which the black whiskers couldn't quite conceal.

"How come you . . . ?"

"Trading. I happened to be at Fetterman when the news got hot. They needed somebody who knew this country well enough to have a chance of finding you, and they claimed that this command had robbed the whole frontier of good scouts. There wasn't a man in the post who had ever been over in this direction."

"We didn't rob just the frontier," a beefy major chuckled. "We even went east for scouts." He glanced toward a tall frontiersman whose long hair hung down over the shoulders of his fringed jacket. "That right, Bill?"

The tall man nodded. "Took me right offa Broadway, Major."

Kirby realized that this must be Bill Cody, the man who had used the name Buffalo Bill to teach the East what the West wanted it to know—or believe.

Gibson broke in again. "You must have neglected your army training, Mase. First lesson of the army, you know; don't volunteer."

Kirby grinned amiably, realizing that this by-play was letting men get rid of some of their tensions. All of them had been badly shaken by the news of the Little Bighorn defeat. "Blame it on Dutch Heilig," he told Gibson. "Dutch knew that I'd spent a lot of time in this part of the country and he spilled his guts to the commander.

They pointed a mountain howitzer at me—and I volunteered."

Gibson suddenly remembered something. "Regrets, gentlemen," he said briskly. "This is Mason Kirby, once lieutenant under Colonel Wessels at old Fort Phil Kearney following the Fetterman blunder. He's had his share of Indian fighting and knows what it's all about."

Kirby saw that the introduction had carried some weight. He was no longer just another civilian who had been pressed into army service. Now he was one of them. They might listen a little more carefully to a man who had once worn the blue.

He acknowledged individual introductions and took his place in the circle that had formed beside the big wagon. In addition to General Merritt there were eight officers present. With Cody, three other civilian scouts, and himself it added up fourteen, every man in the group soberly silent as the brief flurry of joking died away.

General Merritt was brisk in his opening. "My orders are explicit, gentlemen. General Crook is to be reinforced without delay. Instead of returning to Fort Laramie we're to proceed to Fort Fetterman instead, there to pick up supplies and move northward toward General Crook's base camp. I think we will be wise to hold our position here for the night while we make some plans and see that stragglers catch up. We'll proceed in the new direction at four o'clock tomorrow morning. While on the march every officer is to inspect his units and his equipment as carefully as possible so that when we reach Fort Fetterman we'll know exactly what must be done in order to make the next march. Are there any comments on those orders?"

When no reply came he asked, "Now what about the proper route to take? Do any of you know the country well enough to advise me?"

Kirby waited until he saw that none of the other scouts was going to say anything. Then he replied, "I can lay out a general course, sir. I did not come by the direct route, since I didn't know exactly where I might intercept this command, but I'll make a list of landmarks and the like. You'll have no trouble in following it."

"I was through here once," an elderly scout with a sweeping white mustache admitted. "With a mite o' help I kin guide. How's the water in Old Woman Fork? Too deep for wagons?"

"I didn't come that way," Kirby reminded him. "The weather has been pretty dry though. I think you could cross it."

"What other route is there?" General Merritt inquired.

"You could follow the divide and stay away from the larger streams. It'll add miles to the trip and I don't think you'll gain much. I'd favor the shorter haul and depend on the creeks being low enough for fording."

"What's wrong with you bein' guide?" Cody inquired. "You seem to know what you're doin'."

"I'm not going back to Fort Fetterman. I'll go along for one day's march to make sure everything starts right and to get you through the only real bad stretch. Then my temporary job is done. I'm just a civilian, you know." He was a little pleased with himself that he had figured out a way to give himself the time he needed. If Joe Lowry was with the train, he should be able to find him in that length of time.

"That will be the way of it, gentlemen," the commander said with decision. "Have every unit ready to move at four."

"One other thing," Kirby interrupted. "Perhaps you will recall that when I met you I reported seeing a number of Cheyennes who apparently had been watching your movements. I have a feeling that they are now reporting your departure. It could mean a major break by the reservation Indians. They are quite worried over such a possibility at Fort Fetterman. Can anything be done to forestall it?"

Merritt shook his head. "I haven't forgotten it, Mr. Kirby, but I don't see how I can ignore a direct order. When we came out here, I understood that a major part of the year's campaign strategy was to immobilize these Indians around the Red

Cloud Agency. General Sheridan was pretty positive on that point. I still think it's important, but apparently they have changed their opinion at headquarters. Reinforcing General Crook seems to be a more important duty at this point. We have no choice. The orders stand as given."

CHAPTER 9

Kirby wasted no time in rolling into his blankets, most of the command already having done so. Reveille would sound at about three-thirty for the four o'clock march, with breakfast to be cooked at a mid-morning rest halt. The night would be all too short for a man who had been in the saddle all during the previous night.

Still sleep evaded him for some minutes, his mind dwelling on the problem before the regimental commander. General Merritt understood the risk they were running, but his orders were clear and direct. He had to leave Fort Robinson without possible aid and he had to leave the passes of the South Cheyenne unguarded. Crook's need for his troops must be great.

Kirby knew what his own program would be. In the morning he would canvas the wagoners at the morning stop. If Lowry—or anyone who might possibly be Lowry—was with the outfit, then plans would be made on the spot. If it turned out that Lowry had not joined this column then Kirby would cut back toward Fort Robinson. In which case he would not be too much interested in finding Lowry; he would have another kind of errand there. They might need all the help they could get.

It seemed to him that he had not quite shut his eyes when reveille sounded. He ached in every lean muscle, the hard ride after days of inactivity telling on him. It was painful just to scramble out of the blanket but he finally forced himself to do it, knowing that other waking men were moving about at a far brisker pace.

In spite of his pains he knew a sort of nostalgia at the once familiar sounds of the awakening camp. A regiment preparing to march seemed to have a muffled clatter all its own. Kirby recognized it now and wondered at the way his own life had altered. In the old days he had done his full share of complaining about the rigors of frontier duty and the general tenor of army life. Now he knew that he had been missing something ever since he had left it. He wasn't quite sure what it was that he had missed. Certainly it would not have been the physical discomforts, but definitely there was something he could sense without being able to define, perhaps something like comradeship, the feeling of being part of a team. A regiment on active campaign duty became a mighty close knit group if it amounted to anything as a regiment. Kirby decided that the Fifth was such a team and he was a little envious that he could not really be a part of it.

Then he shook it off, telling himself that this was no time for crazy romantic notions. He had to find Lowry as quickly as possible. Or he had to establish that Lowry was not with the Fifth. Then he could hustle on to Fort Robinson. Every time he thought about those Cheyenne scouts watching the column he knew a foreboding. That band of warriors hadn't been watching the Fifth just because they liked to watch cavalry on the march!

Along with Cody and the white mustached scout he took the lead when the column moved out, striking straight west into the path of the moon. The stars were bright enough to suggest that daylight would be hours away instead of merely minutes, so travel was easy enough, the country reasonably flat and free from the gullies and buttes which marked so much of the territory.

Still it was slow work, the column held to the pace of the wagons even though haste had become the order of the day. Crook had been stopped and Custer had been wiped out. The Fifth was needed somewhere to the north, perhaps to stop some kind of counter-attack by the great concentration of Sioux and Cheyennes. On the march they had to recognize the possibility that the war on the Powder might have swept southward. Perhaps even now raiding parties were ranging into this very region. Accordingly skirmishers were thrown out and the regiment advanced almost as though going into hostile country.

Some three hours after dawn the commander called a halt, breakfast fires were lighted, and a substantial breakfast prepared while the horses had a chance to rest and eat the remaining bits of grain and hay left in the supply wagons. Kirby skipped the meal, using the time to ride back along the line of wagons to stare hard at the men who had been riding them. Nowhere could he spot a refugee who fitted the Lowry description. There were men of the right height or weight but none of them happened to have missing teeth. Kirby had to assume that Lowry had not been fitted with dentures. Few men on the frontier were.

When the marching order came, there was still a section of wagons not yet checked, so Kirby abandoned his advance scouting duties, aware by this time that the old fellow with the white mustache really knew the area better than he had been willing to admit. His name was Pop Winans and he had been calling off the landmarks ahead of time since early dawn.

"Straight west until you strike Old Woman Fork," Kirby reminded him casually. "You know the ford better than I do, I imagine. I'm going to cut back along the wagon train and look for a man. Then I'll swing out wide to the south to make sure that no more Cheyennes are trailing us."

There was no argument so he pulled aside, letting the regiment pass. Again he took up his scrutiny of both wagon drivers and refugees. It was hard to judge men's heights when they were hunched on wagon seats, but he could eliminate some and stare harder at the others. He didn't think he had ever seen such a collection of dirty, disheveled men, not even in the Montana gold camps. In addition to the ones who traveled with the wagons there was another detachment straggling along at the rear, some of them on horses and mules but others trudging along wearily afoot. The Fifth's rear guard constantly had to keep prodding them to keep up. They looked beaten and angry but Kirby didn't feel too much sympathy. He felt beaten and angry himself; Joe Lowry wasn't among them.

He sent his horse forward along the slow moving line, overtaking the scouts just about an hour after leaving them. Winans claimed to be having trouble in picking the best route through broken country to reach the passage of Old Woman Fork. Several trails would have been available for the cavalrymen but getting the wagons through was another matter. Kirby took over, leading the way through a narrow cut between two great flat buttes. It was almost a hidden passage, at least from most angles, but it opened into easy country and led straight toward the best ford. Winans declared that he had not even known that the opening existed.

"That's why Kirby came along," Cody said cheerfully. "Every man to his own neck of the woods if you want to know the real important things. Me, I'm kinda lost down this way."

They were still some distance short of the fork when a vidette from the left flank rode up to report dust in the southeast. The word was passed forward and Kirby issued orders. "Winans, you keep picking out trail. Cody and Abe can ride back there with me. If somebody's behind us, we need to know who it is and why."

Nobody argued with him, the understanding being that he was in charge here while he chose to remain with the column. He swung his horse, followed by Cody and the younger scout known as Abe. The trio fanned out a little as they rode, keeping clear of each other's dust and at the same time giving themselves extra chances to find good vantage points for observation.

Cody spotted the dust first and pulled up to look. "One man," he shouted. "And in one big hell of a hurry."

"Hold it here," Kirby shouted in reply. "No need to go meet him. He's heading straight toward us."

The three men closed in toward each other, questions on all three faces. Kirby offered an answer. "I'm guessing the Cheyennes busted out. Just like I called it last night." Then he added with a grin, "I'm not trying to say that I told you so. The rest were all thinking the same thing."

"And us with orders to pull out!" Cody growled. "Now what do we do?"

That was exactly the question which General Merritt had to answer when the dusty rider overtook them. The man proved to be no other than Sergeant "Alabam" Truitt and for once his broad drawl was not so slow. Kirby had called the turn exactly. The Cheyennes were on the warpath. Colonel Stanton, now at Fort Robinson, stated positively that over 800 Cheyenne and Sioux warriors were making war medicine on the reservation and were set to ride north to join the triumphant forces of Sitting Bull, Crazy Horse, and Dull Knife. Reports of Indian successes on the Rosebud and the Little Bighorn had come in promptly and had been too exciting for the peaceful counsels of the old men. Every young warrior who had fretted in idleness while their northern brethren had gone to war now saw a chance to take part in a great Indian success. Some of the older warriors, smarting under old defeats, were joining them. The Cheyennes and remaining Sioux of the Red Cloud Agency were about to offer Sitting Bull 900 fresh warriors.

Again all officers and scouts were called for a hasty council-of-war, but this time the commander did not ask for advice. "All of you know what was said last night," he told them without preliminary. "All of you know what our orders are. I am assuming full responsibility for disregarding those orders, so I do not ask any of you for an opinion which might seem to shift any of that responsibility to you. I propose to turn back at once and attempt to head off the Cheyennes. If any of you object to taking my orders when you know they are in direct disregard of those I have received, I ask you to put those objections in writing immediately and file them with the adjutant. After that I expect every one of you to carry out such orders as I may issue. Is there any comment?"

"Just one, sir," a grizzled company commander growled. "When do we start back?"

Merritt smiled briefly, looking around for further remarks. When none came, he replied, "We move as soon as possible. That means as soon as you can put these orders into effect. Every company commander is to select his best men and horses so as to make up a striking force of 500 men. That force will move out ahead, leaving the poorer mounts for the detachment which will come along with the baggage train. In this case the only baggage wagons will be those carrying ammunition and emergency rations. All other wagons will continue to Fort Fetterman. Arm the teamsters. Along with the sick and the walking wounded they'll have to take care of themselves for the rest of the way. Most of the refugee miners are armed, so they'll be able to defend the wagons if any attack comes. Any questions?"

There were several of them, the most important one being the problem of locating the rebellious Cheyennes. Sergeant Truitt had left Fort Robinson just before dawn and at that time the Cheyennes were still war dancing and doing their usual round of speech making. Colonel Stanton believed that they would leave around midday, thus making a big show of their newly discovered valor.

Another tough one, Kirby decided. Here again was an example of troops going to face aroused warriors. It would have been far better to let them work off their surplus steam and then hit them, but under the circumstances the choice was limited. Maybe they wouldn't be available for any kind of army attack.

He didn't let himself think about the other alternative, that the Cheyennes might strike at the Red Cloud Agency before departing to the north.

"Could we reach Fort Robinson before they break loose?" General Merritt asked, aiming the question at Sergeant Truitt who was on the fringe of the circle.

"No, suh," Truitt said positively. "Ah rode hahd to git heah an' them Cheyennes must be movin' no'th by this time."

"Advise me," the commander requested briefly, this time looking toward the scouts. He had previously made it entirely clear that he would refer matters of time, distance, and trails to the men who were supposed to know. His officers and men were capable enough but they had operated for some time in Arizona, only coming to the Platte and South Cheyenne weeks earlier. They simply didn't know this stretch of chalky country between the Black Hills and the Platte.

Again Kirby found himself on the spot. Cody spelled it out. "We can figure a bit on our back trail, General, but Kirby knows a heap more about this country than any of the rest of us do. And he wasn't just talkin' when he said he knew it. He's been callin' the right turns all mornin'."

Kirby smiled briefly at the inference that the other scouts had been checking up on him. "Nine years since I worked through here, sir," he reminded the commander. "I'll try to remember as many details as possible."

"Thank you . . . Lieutenant." General Merritt was letting him know that his former rank and responsibilities had not been forgotten. "Major Butler, if you'll bring a map I'd like Lieutenant Kirby to point out what he considers to be the trail these Indians are most like to take."

A map was ready without delay, Kirby recognizing it as one of the early attempts which must have dated back to the Carrington campaign. The main trails between the Platte and the Red Cloud Agency were sketched in with some accuracy, obviously at a later date than the original. Otherwise it was vague, lacking in almost everything.

Except for the main trail between Fort Robinson and Fort Laramie there had never been much travel in the region and no one had bothered to bring maps up-to-date.

"We're at about this spot," he told them, placing a finger on one of the empty places. "Perhaps 60 miles or a bit more east of Fort Fetterman and almost as far northwest of the Agency. Obviously there is no possible chance of making the fantastic time Sergeant Truitt did. We can't hope to get back to Fort Robinson in time to stop the Indians. Even if we arrived after a forced march we'd have exhausted men and horses. The Indians could simply run away from us—if they didn't choose to attack."

"And what would be the chances of intercepting them at some other point?"

"Maybe it could be done. We know they're all excited, anxious to join Sitting Bull and Crazy Horse. That means they'll head north by the best and most direct route. There's a much used Indian trail that runs north from the Agency past the headwaters of Hat Creek, crosses Warbonnet Creek at a ford and passes through a gap in the line of hills north of the Warbonnet. From there it goes straight to the South Cheyenne and crosses just below the mouth of Saco Creek. After that it's a straightaway shot to the Powder." He was tracing it with a finger nail as he spoke.

"We crossed that trail yesterday, General,"

Cody remarked. "Just before we turned up Saco."

"How long ago was that?"

"Two days march, more or less. Without wagons we could make it back to the crossin' in half the time."

Merritt's voice had sharpened as he asked, "You agree with that, Kirby?"

"Sounds fair enough to me, sir."

"That's our move then. Marching orders just as I gave them a few minutes ago. We're heading for that line of hills between the Cheyenne and Warbonnet Creek. I'm going to keep those Cheyennes from joining Sitting Bull if it's humanly possible. All of you know quite well how much depends on it."

Kirby didn't bother to protest the obvious fact that at this point he no longer had any obligation to the army. His volunteer service was at an end, and he was completely at liberty to turn toward Fort Robinson at his own convenience. But he would not have missed this next move for anything. Merritt's success or failure might determine the whole course of the Indian war. What had happened on the Rosebud and the Little Bighorn might be repeated again and again if the Cheyennes were permitted to swell the ranks of the victorious Sioux. This little backwash of the campaign might prove to be a turning point, and he didn't want to miss it.

Company commanders hastened to the business

of picking their best men and mounts, the rising tension indicating that the men were eager, more than willing to undertake the grueling ride and certain dangers ahead. The shock of the Custer story had gradually turned into a grim anger. The Fifth was going to have its chance to strike a blow in revenge for the Seventh.

Daylight was fading when they started into the northeast, aiming for Saco Creek in as straight a line as possible. With any luck they might cut off several miles from the westbound trip. At first they had been headed toward Fort Laramie and had then turned northwest when Kirby met them. Now they could strike almost due east instead of riding two legs of a triangle. Darkness fell before they could find Saco, and then it took a bit of blundering in the dark to locate the ford. They rested horses on the far bank and moved on just before moonrise.

When the moon came up, the travel became easier and Kirby calculated that they would make the South Cheyenne on time unless the Indians had ridden northward sooner than he calculated. If they had done the usual bit of dancing and making medicine, they would still be far enough south to be intercepted.

At dawn there was a rather lengthy halt, the scouts going forward while breakfast was being cooked. There was no sign of Indians in the area, so the march was resumed at a cautious pace now because of the need for keeping horses from complete exhaustion.

In mid-afternoon they reached the South Cheyenne, the column crawling slowly now as fatigue began to take its toll. Finally General Merritt called in the scouts for another consultation. The race against time had become a struggle with exhaustion, and it was becoming clear that sheer enthusiasm was not going to be enough. Men were sleeping in their saddles, and the horses were stumbling badly.

Again the final decision was thrust upon Kirby and this time he felt a little more confident in making it, having been working things out in his mind all along the line of march.

"I figure that we have about six hours march ahead of us to reach the gap in the ridge north of Warbonnet Creek. If we assume that the Cheyennes didn't leave the Agency until this morning—which is quite likely, in view of their lengthy medicine making—then it seems definite that they didn't reach Warbonnet Creek yet. I think they'll camp a few miles to the south and make their crossing tomorrow morning. I suggest that we halt right here and get all the rest we can between now and ten o'clock tonight. From here on the going is fairly good and we'll have moonlight by midnight. If we can be in position north of the Warbonnet at four o'clock tomorrow morning, we can hit them hard when they try to cross at the ford. And we'll have to really hit them; nothing else will take the ginger out of them at this stage of the game."

"Suppose you've guessed wrong and they've already crossed?" Merritt asked.

"Then we're already too late. Nothing we do will be any good because we're too weary to do any chasing."

"He's right, General," Cody put in. "We got to dump all of our eggs in one basket. If we can block 'em off at this ford we still got to be fresh enough to do some fightin'. Eight or 900 crazy young Cheyenne bucks ain't goin' to be no easy meat."

"Suppose they spot us and ride around? Our horses probably couldn't even cut them off."

"We'll have a good chance of going undetected," Kirby told him. "The Warbonnet flows along the southeast side of a line of hills. If the command remains out of sight behind the hills until the Cheyennes attempt their crossing, we'll have them foul. It'll be the kind of ambush the Cheyennes themselves would like to set up."

"Sounds right to me," Winans agreed suddenly after having kept silent from the beginning. "I remember them hills. It'll work fine."

"It had better work!" Merritt growled. "And I'm not just thinking about my own skin. I'll undoubtedly be court martialed for disobedience to orders if we don't pull off something pretty impressive, but that's not the important thing. If these Cheyennes get through, others will try to follow. The whole territory will be a bloody mess."

He barked new orders at the officers. Kirby's plan was to be put into execution. The regiment would rest again and push on at ten o'clock. Tomorrow would tell whether they had wasted all this effort.

CHAPTER 10

Kirby did not need to call upon his knack of going to sleep. The accumulating weariness scarcely permitted him to crawl into a blanket roll, lame muscles forgotten in spite of their aches. He didn't even wait to eat any supper. Ten o'clock came all too soon and he stumbled through the business of getting into the saddle again, knowing that most of the men around him were almost as tired. Probably they were a little more hardened to it, but all of them simply had to be aching from weariness. Still they set out smartly enough, officers having taken a few extra minutes to check weapons and ammunition.

Winans and Kirby took the lead during the night. They were the only ones who really had any knowledge of the country so it seemed to be their job, the other scouts dozing in their saddles with the knowledge that their turn would come soon enough. Laying an ambush for a gang of clever Cheyennes was going to take all the frontier cunning they could muster.

Kirby's timetable worked out perfectly. At a quarter to four they found the Indian trail where it came up through the break in the hills. The moonlight was plenty bright enough to tell them that no sizable band had passed the spot recently.

"We're in time—if this is the trail they're

taking," Kirby muttered half aloud. "Send the word back and I'll have a look at the ford."

Everything seemed quiet along the creek and he could find no reason to believe that the Cheyennes were camped very close to it. Then he returned to find that General Merritt had come forward to peer into the first grays of dawn in an effort to map the strategy. Kirby could point out the salient features and again the commander did not hesitate. Within a few minutes orders were going back to company commanders.

The troopers were to dismount and wait, keeping well behind the line of buttes which flanked the creek on its left hand bank. They would be completely screened from any Indians coming up from the south and they could recoup their vigor while they cleaned dust from their weapons. A company would hold each flank to prevent a crossing at some part of the stream other than the usual ford, but the bulk of the regiment was to form immediately behind the gap in the ridge, ready to pour through in a charge when the command should be given. General Merritt, his staff, couriers, and scouts would climb the ridge and wait for daylight to tell them whether they would turn the ford of Warbonnet Creek into a battleground.

Faint tinges of red were fading the eastern stars by the time these dispositions were made, Kirby settling himself just behind the crest of the ridge so that he could have a good view of the rolling country south of the creek without exposing anything but his head. Other scouts took similar positions, but the staff officers and couriers remained on the lower slopes, snatching moments of rest in the manner of men starved for sleep. Nobody was in a mood to talk, even if it would have been prudent to do so. A mere matter of minutes now would tell them whether their big gamble was going to pay off.

Kirby felt hopeful. He had lived with these Cheyennes long enough to know something of their habits and he didn't believe that he had made any wrong calculations. They would come through this gap—and they certainly had not made it yet.

The dawn seemed to be taking its own good time about turning into day, but eventually the pale yellows of the sandy wasteland began to show definite outlines. The swales beyond Warbonnet Creek were empty of life. Nowhere could the watchers detect any sign of life, Indian or otherwise.

Kirby had noticed that a soldier was climbing toward him but he paid little attention until a familiar drawl came softly, "Yo' think we missed 'em, Mistah Kuhby?" "Alabam" Truitt's red-rimmed eyes peered anxiously from behind a three-days growth of beard.

Kirby shook his head. "I think they're over

there in the hills some little distance. They didn't pass through here, that's for sure!"

"Supposin' they attacked the Agency instead o' ridin' no'th? Mebbe we-uns is makin' a bad mistake."

"That's the risk we've got to take. If they don't show soon we'll take a look. Then maybe we'll have to ride again. South, this time, and in a bigger hurry than ever."

Truitt nodded his understanding. "Mebbe fo'ty good men at the Agency. Wahned and ready. They could hold out quite a spell."

"Good." Then he thought of something. "How did you know where to find this column so quickly? You made one hell of a ride to do it the way you did."

"Only left 'em a couple o' days befoah. Paid off these heah troopahs befoah we headed fo' the Agency."

Kirby let that sink in. He had wasted an opportunity. Assuming that Colonel Stanton and his escort had gone directly to the Red Cloud Agency, he had failed to follow up his first hunch just because there had been a day's delay. Actually he could have reached the place at least a day ahead of the paymaster, probably while Colonel Stanton was still paying off the men of the Fifth Cavalry.

"Yo'd ha' got him," Truitt said suddenly. "He was theah all the time."

"Who?"

"That brush-ape of a Lowry. I been pickin' up the whole tale, heah and theah. It ain't none o' mah business, Ah know, but Mis' Nell seem lahk she wanted somebody to talk to about it."

They talked in low tones for a few minutes, Kirby discovering that Truitt indeed knew the whole miserable story. The sergeant also hinted that many men in the Fetterman garrison suspected the truth. Everyone seemed to know that the army wanted Lowry and that Kirby wanted Lowry. They were not quite sure why Mrs. Perry was so anxious to find the man first.

"I'm not too sure I still want him," Kirby said quietly. "First I tell myself I'll kill him if I have a chance, but then I don't give a damn whether I get him or not."

Truitt grinned. "The lady was hopin' it'd work out thataway. But yo' ain't got no chance. The ahmy's got him. He come a runnin' when the Cheyennes got afteh him."

"What Cheyennes?"

"Mostly the old men. Seems as how they blame Lowry foah stahtin' the young bucks into trouble by sellin' 'em whiskey. So he went behind bahs instead o' lettin' the old chiefs take his haiah."

"Could be he's not safe even there any longer," Kirby said gloomily. "If the Cheyennes decided to break loose, there's better than a fair chance that they tried to wipe out Fort Robinson at the first uproar."

"Don't git all spooked up," Truitt advised. "Countin' the paymasteh's escoht theah must be fohty good men at the Agency. They know wheah they stand and they ain't goin' to git caught nappin'. Anyway it don't look lahk them Cheyennes would ever make a pass at the place. Yo' got to remembeh that it's only the young ones that's itchin' to git rough. They'll be kinda lahk a bunch a' young whippeh-snappehs runnin' away f'm home. They ain't a-goin' to hang around wheah theah pappys kin git tough with 'em. The old Injuns might even fight foah the Agency. Anyhow Ah don't figgah as how the folks theah at the Agency is goin' to be in any real dangeh."

Kirby forced a small grin. "You make it sound pretty good, Sarge. And generally you've had things figured out mighty close to right. I'll hope you're running true to form."

"She'll be safe enough," Truitt went on, as though reading Kirby's mind. Then he pulled a wry grin as he caught the quick glance that was aimed at him. "Ah didn't mean to git pussonal, but somehow eve'ybody's kinda got it figgahed out that the pair of yo' is kinda aimin' foah yo know what."

"Mrs. Perry tell you that?" Kirby demanded.
"No, suh."
"Did she hint at it?"

"Kinda admitted it when Ah mentioned that it was kinda common opinion around the foht. She's a real fine lady, suh. Can't remember when Ah evah saw a cuteh one."

"You sound like Mrs. Heilig," Kirby growled, trying to sound disgusted. It wasn't easy to sound disgusted when he was thinking about Nell. But he didn't have much time to think about it. There was a trailer of dust several miles to the southwest.

General Merritt climbed to the ridge top to stare with the others. "I'm afraid we kicked the wrong spot, Mr. Kirby. They seem to be making for a crossing farther upstream. They'll pass behind us."

Kirby stared hard and shook his head. "No break in the hills up that way. I don't believe Indians are making that dust."

Abe's eyes must have been sharper than any of the others for he called across, "It's the ammunition wagons. Looks like they've been rollin' all night."

"Damn!" General Merritt exclaimed. "Why did Hall have to pick this particular time to get so damned efficient? If any Indians move toward the ford now, they'll see the train through the gaps in the ridge. At least they'll see dust and suspect that we've got troops on hand."

Everyone knew what he had in mind. The Cheyennes had the advantage of superior numbers and fresher horses; the only good chance of beating them back was to catch them by surprise. Now that surprise was lost!

"Get a man back there in a hurry!" the commander ordered. "Tell Lieutenant Hall to pull up behind the hills and out of sight from the south. Explain what we're trying to do. Warn them that they may be attacked."

After the first angry disappointment Kirby began to feel a sort of sympathy for Lieutenant Hall. The regimental quartermaster had made an impossible march with those wagons in a valiant effort to keep supplies close to the troops. Now his effort was turning out to be an embarrassment that might be actually disastrous. Sometimes a man couldn't seem to be right for being wrong.

Then he saw the movement in the hills to the south. "Here come the Cheyennes," he warned. "Keep down. We may get a crack at them yet."

Merritt issued new orders and a second courier hastened down the hill to his horse. Two companies were to be ready to ride back to the support of the supply wagons if the Indians should swing wide to attack at that point. All other orders remained in force.

The tense expectancy of early dawn had now turned into something like dismay. If the Cheyennes avoided the ford, scenting a trap, there would be no catching them. The cavalry horses had been resting, but they would still be too nearly exhausted to have any chance of overtaking the relatively fresh Indian ponies.

Sergeant Truitt voiced the only optimistic note, murmuring in Kirby's ear, "Looks like they didn't waste no time at the Agency, Mistah Kuhby."

"I thought of that. And with a great deal of relief. But what do we do about it now?"

"They're sendin' scouts forward," Cody called out. "Now we'll get an idea of what they're up to." The veteran plainsman would reassume his duty as chief scout now. Kirby had been guide, but Cody was the man who had fought the Cheyennes before. Interpreting their moves for the commander would be his responsibility.

Apparently the Cheyenne leaders had seen either the wagons or their dust and were puzzled by what they saw. The main force of warriors halted some 400 yards short of the long slope which led down to the creek bottom, and now a file of riders swung wide to the west in an apparent effort to learn what was going on across the stream and behind the line of bluffs.

"We may hit them yet if they see the wagons and think they're only lightly escorted. The big thing now is to make sure that none of their scouts see our man back of this ridge." General Merritt was evidently planning for all sorts of possibilities.

At that point a messenger climbed the slope to where the commander and the scouts were peering out across the creek. "Captain Miles reports, sir, that two men are coming up along the creek. He thinks they're couriers from Lieutenant Hall. They missed meeting the man who rode back to pass the orders to the wagons because they seem to have cut through toward the creek side of the hills. At least we couldn't see 'em any more from back there."

Every eye turned upstream. The bend of the valley prevented any real observation of the near side flats, but presently they could see the heads of two riders coming downstream along the left bank. Another blunder for which no one could reasonably be blamed. Lieutenant Hall wanted to let his commander know that the wagons had made excellent time during the night and he had sent messengers to overtake the regiment. Now those messengers had decided to ride along the creek—just in time to come under the direct observation of Indian scouts they would not know about.

"The Cheyennes have spotted them," Kirby stated quietly. "They're turning a bit now, spreading out. They can't seem to make up their minds whether to take a crack at the soldiers or to go on across for a look at that wagon dust."

Meanwhile the two troopers seemed to be completely unconscious of the attention they were getting. Their position in the shallow valley did not permit them to see the main force of

Cheyennes, the scouting party so much closer to them, or the cavalry units almost directly ahead. They hadn't realized their danger any more than they appreciated what a mess they were making of some very careful plans.

The Cheyenne scouts seemed to be baffled by what they saw and perhaps suspecting a trap. "They're puzzled," Kirby stated with some confidence. "They figure this regiment is far off to the west and they can't imagine what a couple of troopers are doing down along the Warbonnet or what that wagon dust may mean. We'll have to see whether curiosity, caution, or war lust controls them."

The Cheyenne scouts had bunched again after starting to spread out, apparently talking it over. The main body still waited in the middle distance, clearly not aware of what had disturbed their scouting party.

Cody nodded at Kirby's words. "I think they'll try for a couple o' scalps. It's in Injun nature to think that way. General, suppose'n I take some men along with me and ride back along the north side o' the hills to the break that shows beyond that broken topped butte. We ought to reach there just about the time them troopers hit the other side, and maybe just about the time the Injun scout party takes a crack at 'em."

"The whole Cheyenne force will see you."

"But they won't see many of us. Like Kirby

says, they don't figure as how there's a regiment here. It'll look like wagon guards. Maybe we'll even draw 'em on."

"Go ahead. Otherwise those troopers are going to be slaughtered before our very eyes."

They were planning it properly, Kirby thought. Already the Cheyenne scout party was starting to make its move. They were going to ignore the dust and the wagons while they took a couple of quick scalps. That would be big medicine for a war party just starting out. Indian superstition wouldn't let them ignore such a fine opportunity.

And Cody had named the proper spot. The creek was shallow at that point, a little draw coming down to the ford from the south side. The Cheyenne could come through it and be at the ford before the unsuspecting troopers could see them. Cody's plan of riding across the ridge to defend the messengers had the same kind of advantage. He and his men would be concealed until almost the last moment and then could break out at the critical spot along the creek. It might alarm the main body of Cheyennes, but it had to be tried. If the two men along the creek managed to break away from the first attack, they would lead their pursuers straight into the ambush. Either the scouts would see the main body of soldiers waiting there or they would be gobbled up by the overanxious men of the Fifth.

Sixteen Indians would spring a trap intended for 900.

The commander had evidently seen it just that way. "Take a squad from the nearest company," he told Cody. "Play it as cautiously as possible. We'll try to make them think that the train's advance guard has stepped in to save the two men. Warn the commanders below of what we're doing."

"Right, sir. With a bit of luck we might even bait the main force to come along and try to wipe us out."

"No officers, mind you," Merritt called after him. "We don't want this to look like anything but small business."

Kirby was following Cody down the slope. No one paid any particular attention to him as the observers were so intent on watching the maneuvers of the Cheyenne scouts as the Indians worked around to hit the draw it had been so certain they would use for their approach.

Cody was picking his men from the nearest company when Kirby swung into his saddle and rode across to join him. "Seems like I won't look like an officer," he grinned, glancing down at his battered and dusty garb. "Mind if I come along?"

"Glad to have you. Between us we'll sure as hell keep this from lookin' too fancy." He went on with the business of selecting his men, the company commander leaving it entirely up to him. After those weeks of scouting it was pretty clear that quite an understanding had grown up between the scouts and the regiment. Cody knew which men to trust, and the company commanders were willing to let him do the choosing.

Brief minutes later the little party was on its way, fourteen troopers riding in twos behind the scouts. They climbed the ridge far enough so that they would still be below the skyline and then worked along its side until they struck the low spot Cody had selected. There was just time for Cody to make a final observation and then he waved them on. They pounded through the little notch and down into the creek valley just as the Cheyennes started their charge from beyond the creek.

Kirby let a swift grin cross his lips as he realized what these two blundering troopers must be thinking. One minute they had been riding along in apparently peaceful sunshine, and without warning all hell had broken loose around them. Cheyennes were splashing headlong through the shallows, and other horsemen were coming out of the hills on the other side. They did not wait to identify either party, simply spurring their horses hard and making a break for the main pass which they could see ahead of them.

It was the Cheyennes, however, who seemed most surprised. Several of them were halfway across the Warbonnet, the others not yet into the stream. The Indians in the creek pulled up to fire at the oncoming troopers, but the others turned tail and fled in sudden panic. There was a brief clatter of arms as the soldiers drove into the water from their side, their shooting far better than that of the Cheyennes. One trooper suffered a flesh wound in the thigh, but three Cheyennes were killed outright. Then the Indians were in full retreat.

"Follow the messengers!" Cody yelled. "Make it look as if we're just as scared as they are. Maybe we can draw the bastards back for another shot at us."

Almost as he issued the order the Cheyennes were coming back again. Now that the moment of surprise was over, they could see that the force opposing them was about equal to their own strength. And the warriors who had first retreated now had an added incentive; they had to make up for their show of cowardice.

"They're mad now," Kirby yelled. "They'll be tough. Hit 'em hard."

The little band of troopers swung around out of their pretended retreat and once more rode to meet the Indians at the shallow spot. "Don't let any of 'em get across the ridge," Cody shouted warningly. "We've got to make the rest of the crowd come on. When they do, we retreat through the main gap."

The two parties closed grimly this time, hand

to hand fights breaking out briefly and then breaking as the Indians tried their usual hit and run tactics. Kirby shot a warrior off his pony at short range, but then the fight swung away from him, showers of spray thrown up by thrashing horses making it almost impossible to know what was actually happening. He pulled back toward the creek bank to get a better look at the skirmish and immediately saw what was happening. The scout party was not actually trying to force the passage of the stream but was fighting a delaying action, waiting for the main body of Cheyennes to come up.

Two men joined him, both nursing minor wounds, so he sent them off toward the pass. "Make it look like you're on the run," he snapped. "And tell them to get ready—if they don't already know what's happening."

He hoped they wouldn't have to delay their own retreat too long. With the whole Cheyenne force coming up it would get pretty hot for troops fighting a retreating action. Still it was what had been planned; the Cheyennes had to be lured into the ambush.

Then came an odd diversion which threatened the whole plan. A chief in full war regalia chose that moment to hail Cody, his English clear enough as he shouted across the stream. He called the famous scout by his Indian name and challenged him to single combat. "I know you,

Pa-ho-has-ka," the Cheyenne yelled. "Come and fight with one who knows how to kill such as you!" With the challenge the chief swung in front of his followers who had drawn back from their dashing attacks, riding his pony in a tight little circle while he repeated the challenge.

"Look out, Bill," Kirby warned. "This can be just a dodge to hold us here while the rest of that mob gets into range."

"Likely so," Cody replied. "But it's also real serious business when a chief plays games like this. If I can knock him over, it'll have a mighty healthy effect on the rest of 'em."

He swung to shout a command at the men who had followed him. "Don't let that big crowd close in on you. Fall back slow and draw 'em on. Lead 'em into the pass if you can. Meanwhile I'll see if I can't teach this varmint a lesson."

He whirled his mount and drove into the stream, heading straight toward the boasting Cheyenne. The Indian stopped his circling and met the attack, both men firing their weapons at almost the same instant. The Cheyenne missed entirely but Cody's bullet killed the Indian pony, sending the gaudily painted warrior sprawling. He rolled acrobatically in water that was only two or three inches deep and came up with his rifle in his hand. At the same moment Cody's horse stepped into a hole and fell hard.

That put the antagonists on foot and within a

few feet of each other. Since they were now quite a distance from either lot of supporters, it was now definitely the individual duel the Indian had demanded.

  Kirby started into the creek but suddenly pulled up again. Those Cheyennes were getting pretty close now. Since the big objective was to draw them into an ambush, he didn't want to start a general brawl in the middle of Warbonnet Creek. That might mean the death of every soldier in the party and at the same time spoil the main strategy. Cody would have to handle his battle as best he could.

  At that moment he saw that Cody was doing all right. Again the two duelists fired simultaneously and again the Cheyenne missed. Cody wasn't the man to miss at such range and his bullet felled the Indian. With a bound the veteran scout was upon his enemy, using his knife to finish the bloody job and to scalp his victim.

  It was an action calculated to infuriate the watching savages and it almost cost Cody his life. Kirby was the only white man near him as the soldiers had started to withdraw according to orders. Some of the Cheyenne scouting party came charging across the creek farther downstream than Cody's position and above the retreating soldiers. Kirby fired twice into the charging ranks but then pulled back up the slope of the ridge. At the same time the troopers saw what was happening and, without orders, turned back to help the men who were about to be cut off. By that time the main force of Cheyennes had come close to the creek. In a matter of seconds they would be charging across to throw an overwhelming attack on the little handful of whites.

Kirby swore under his breath as he reloaded. This diversion was going to be costly. The ambush was wrecked and they might all lose their lives.

CHAPTER 11

For brief seconds the little fight raged as violently as in its opening flurry, the Cheyenne scouts trying to cut off Cody and the troopers battling desperately to give him time to get clear. Again the threshing horses threw so much water around that it was hard to tell just what was happening, but, when Kirby had emptied his six-gun once more, he knew that Cody was back on dry land. He also knew that the main Cheyenne force was about to throw overwhelming numbers against the little handful of picked troopers. Some of their more ardent warriors had already crossed the creek, directly in the line of retreat which the men were supposed to use.

At that instant a bugle blared the agitating note of the charge and blue clad horsemen began to pour out of the gap downstream. General Merritt had decided to rescue his men rather than to try to make good on his ambush plans. The Fifth was wheeling out into the creek bed at a headlong pace, men who had waited anxiously for hours now seeing their chance to strike that vengeful blow they had been planning all night.

The surprise attack was almost as effective as a true ambush would have been. Some 800 Cheyennes, their morale already affected by the death of one of their leaders, didn't quite know what to do when they found themselves attacked thus on a flank. Some of them were caught in midstream, others already across. The warriors pressing on down the far slope were the last to realize what was happening, and by that time the vanguard was trying to retreat, the result being a tangle of Indian ponies which effectively kept the chiefs from getting any kind of resistance organized. A few shots were fired from either side, but then the Cheyennes broke and fled. Before the angry troopers of the Fifth could get within decent carbine range, the Cheyennes were in disorderly retreat, heading for the Red Cloud Agency as fast as they could get clear of blundering companions.

Panic seemed to spread through the Cheyenne ranks, and the scouts along the creek didn't waste many seconds in joining their fleeing companions. Cody was mounted again by that time and he shouted his little band into action. "Come on, boys. We've done our share but we can do more. Here's one for Custer!"

He was waving the bloody Cheyenne scalp over his head as he shouted, for the moment as much of a savage as any of the panic-stricken warriors on the other side of the creek. He led his detachment across at a gallop, taking the right flank as the Fifth fanned out for the chase. Bugles sang again, and the charge was repeated over and over. General Merritt had been quick to see the psychological advantage and he was pushing it for all it was worth. Indians on the run would hate those bugles, but they would be afraid to turn back into the face of the oncoming troopers.

Kirby wondered about the possibilities, keeping up with the chase and trying to reload as he urged his mount forward. It would be a great thing to be able to chase these Indians all the way back to the Agency. They would never be able to work up any effective war talk again if they were forced to run home with their tails between their legs. The question was whether the troop horses could stand such a pace. They had been fed and they had been resting for a couple of hours, but there were just too many miles behind them.

The Indians pulled away quickly as the cavalry mounts quickly showed their weariness. Cody rode close to Kirby and yelled, "Swing across and find the general. See what he's got in mind. We oughta chase 'em as far as we can. Teach 'em a damned good lesson."

A staff officer was already riding to answer that question and suggestion. The pursuit was to be pressed as far as the condition of men and horses made it possible. One company was being diverted to round up the abandoned pony herd, but the rest of the regiment was to keep pressure on the retreating Indians. Keep them moving, was the general order. Don't give them a chance to recover their wits or to make any kind of stand.

Kirby went back to relay the message, grinning wearily as he told Cody. "Fine one I am to do any chasing," he said. "I'll likely fall asleep in the saddle—if the horse doesn't fall asleep and dump me out."

Somehow he kept going, as did the rest of the pursuing force. There was no longer any dash in it but the general idea was the same as it had been, the only difference being the slower pace. The discomfited Cheyennes kept just out of carbine range and the troopers pushed on just hard enough to keep the Indians moving. The chase had become a plodding sort of game in which the Fifth attempted to save tired horses as much as possible and still keep the abashed Indians from recovering their morale.

"We're really seein' somethin', gents," Cody remarked during one of the long straightaway rides across open country. "They're not digger Injuns up there ahead of us. They're the Fightin' Cheyennes. I've been in a few campaigns out here, but I never saw anything like this before. We're herdin' 'em back to their pens like they was a bunch of sheep."

In spite of his fatigue Kirby had been marveling at the same thing. There had been plenty of Indian fights on the frontier in which the troops had driven Indians in retreat, but he was sure that there had never been anything quite like this. A strong force of warriors, excited by the usual opening ceremonies of war dancing and making medicine, had fled in panic before the attack of a less numerous army unit. Not only had they fled, but they were making no attempt to do any of the things which defeated Indians commonly did.

"We better keep our eyes skinned," Winans growled a little later. "This ain't in Injun nature. Likely as not there's more of the devils down this way a piece. We could git ourselves in an Injun ambush instead of us gettin' them in our'n."

Again it appeared that General Merritt was thinking straight. A staff officer appeared, warning against the very risk Winans had mentioned and asking that Kirby and Cody leave the flank and come to his wagon.

As they approached they saw that he was still riding the jolting ambulance. Kirby wondered why. The general was a good horseman and had done his share of campaigning in the saddle. To use a wagon now seemed odd.

Then he realized the purpose. Inside the wagon two staff officers were doing practically a navigating job, checking a compass against the rough maps which they had spread on the floor of the vehicle. General Merritt motioned toward them. "I feel like the skipper on the quarterdeck," he smiled, "but I'm trying to figure this out. Am I right in thinking that these Indians are running straight for home?"

"That's exactly it, I think," Kirby told him.

"We're all puzzled by it. We've never seen Cheyennes act so much like a herd of cattle—and without actually being hurt very badly. They couldn't have lost more than a dozen men back there on the Warbonnet."

"Two dangers I'm trying to look out for," the commander told them. "I want to keep the pressure on, but I don't want to kill our horses or let my men run into any kind of trap."

"I reckon the worst risk is behind us, General," Cody told him. "If there's another Cheyenne party in the region, they'd have easy pickin's back there. We've been losing stragglers all along the line as horses play out. There's a company tryin' to hold the Injun pony herd and there's the ammunition wagons. We must be strung out for fifteen miles."

"I've passed warnings to all," Merritt told him. "The wagons are to keep following, picking up men as they overtake them. By this time they ought to have a substantial, if tired, guard. The men with the pony herd will try to stay ahead of the wagons. Meanwhile we push; it's our only possibility."

"My sentiments exactly," the scout nodded. "Maybe we don't know it yet, but maybe we're seein' one of the damnedest Injun fights that ever happened."

There was cautious agreement on that. None of them could be sure that the Cheyenne demoralization was as complete as it appeared to be, but on the surface this was beginning to shape up as a complete disaster for the tribesmen. They had not been hit too hard so far as casualties were concerned, but they had retreated so precipitately and so far that it would shatter tribal morale for a good many years to come.

It took all day, with men dropping out all along the way, but finally a bone-tired remnant of the Fifth Cavalry drove their crestfallen enemies right on to the reservation. The retreating warriors simply stopped running and huddled helplessly as the cavalrymen, now badly outnumbered, came up to them. Almost a thousand Cheyennes simply looked forlorn and helpless while a third of their number of white troopers herded them about like cattle. Kirby knew a sense of deep satisfaction through his weariness. It would take mighty strong medicine to get these humiliated Indians on the warpath again.

"Funny thing about Injuns," Cody remarked as they dismounted behind the picket line that had been promptly set up. "Just opposite from a white man where pride's concerned. If any army crowd had behaved the way the Cheyennes did today, they'd be the toughest bunch in the service as soon as they'd caught their breath. Every man of 'em would be fair bustin' to get even with somebody and take the bad taste out of his mouth. Injuns don't think that way. While they're full o' brags, they're tough, but let somebody take the heart out of 'em and they stay licked a long time. This bunch o' Cheyennes will be plumb peaceful for quite a spell."

"About eight years," Kirby said thoughtfully.

"How's that? Don't tell me you got it scheduled like that!"

Kirby's smile was grim in the evening darkness. "That's how long it took for them to get over the Wagon Box and Hayfield fights. If we're lucky the Warbonnet may last a little longer."

"Could be. Now if somebody up along the Little Bighorn will take some of the cockiness out of Sitting Bull and Crazy Horse we might see an end to the whole bloody mess."

It was a reminder that General Merritt's victorious troops had no business being at the Red Cloud Agency. They were supposed to be on their way north to take a hand in the difficult job of handling those triumphant Sioux. By the same token Mason Kirby wasn't doing anything very practical by sitting around to gloat over the Warbonnet victory. He had his own affairs to think about—and for the first time he might actually be within striking distance of Joe Lowry. The trouble was that he could scarcely keep his eyes open. As soon as the chase was actually over, he had practically fallen from the saddle, sore muscles, weary bones, and raw skin reminding him that he had done a month's riding almost without sleep and in a period of about three days. He was in no condition to try conclusions with a man like Lowry.

A staff officer found him while he was thinking about the problem. General Merritt wanted to see him. At first he had a feeling that the commander wanted some other service from him and he was primed to refuse, but it turned out to be quite another matter. In the midst of the triumph the general could not forget that he had gone exactly contrary to orders in taking the Fifth to the Warbonnet crossing. Reports in great detail would have to be made and Merritt wanted a formal statement from Kirby. As a civilian and a man who knew the country his opinion might be valuable.

"After what happened I don't think anybody at headquarters is going to make much of a fuss," Kirby said with a chuckle. "No one in his right mind can think that you did anything that wasn't exactly right and necessary."

General Merritt frowned. "You were a lieutenant, I believe. Right?"

"Yes, sir."

"Then you ought to know that headquarters is full of men who are not in their right minds. All lieutenants are sure of that." The frown faded into a smile as he made his joke, but then he added, "I'm mighty grateful, sir. My own report will give you full credit for finding us so promptly and also for the additional volunteer service which proved so helpful. And I'll not be giving you a good reputation just so your statement will carry added weight on my behalf; I really appreciate what you did. If there's anything I can do for you, just name it."

"Done," Kirby said promptly. "When you meet the Agent see if you can find out what has happened to a couple of people I'm concerned about. One of them is a Mrs. Helen Perry. The other is a whiskey runner and general thug named Lowry. Joe Lowry. I've got to find them, but I'm too doggone tired to move."

"Take a nap," Merritt advised. "I'm going in to the Agency in a few minutes. As soon as I've made arrangements for leaving the place in proper order, I'll have to be moving out again but I'll see what I can do about your errand."

"Thanks. The man is probably in jail. You can find out the truth while I'd be getting pushed around from one clerk to another."

Still he did not find that sleep came easily. His eyes burned, but now that he could think about either Nell or Lowry he couldn't give up to mere weariness. He had to decide what he proposed to do—assuming that he would have a chance to make a decision for himself.

Then he discovered that he had been forgetting his best source of information. Sergeant Truitt appeared at scout camp where Kirby was trying to fall asleep, his approach cautious until he saw that Kirby was not actually sleeping. Then he moved in with a crooked grin showing in the firelight.

"Got me some info'mation, Mistah Kuhby," he announced in a whisper. "Them polecats Ah left on the job heah kept account o' stock. Seems as how youah business is in raht good shape."

Kirby was up and listening. He fired his questions crisply, but the story was just about what Truitt had made it in his first guesses. Lowry had ducked a scalping party of older Cheyennes, choosing jail by comparison. He was to be taken to Laramie under guard for trial. Selling liquor to reservation Indians was a pretty serious matter—particularly this year. The military authorities would probably dish out a pretty severe sentence.

"Now what yo' had in mind foah him," Truitt said in a low voice, "but it ought to make things a mite easieh between yo' and the lady."

"Dammit!" Kirby snapped. "Does everybody and all his relatives have to play cupid for me? Who ever said I was trying to . . . ?"

Truitt chuckled a trifle uneasily. "Kinda seems like it's one o' them things," he shrugged. "Every male old enough to look is plumb jealous of yo'."

Kirby settled himself determinedly into his blanket roll. "Tell them to mind their own damned business," he growled.

There was a moment or two of silence, but then

he opened his eyes again to ask, "Is Mrs. Perry all right?"

The Truitt grin broadened. "She's fine. They didn't have a bit o' trouble outa this mess."

"No? Then you were right about the Indians behaving like runaways."

"Ah had it all sahzed up," Truitt admitted with due modesty.

He told the story in his own rambling fashion. Colonel Stanton had insisted on full precautions for the post as soon as word of the Cheyenne dancing came to them. The handful of troopers on garrison duty were supplemented by Stanton's escort and the armed employees. Everyone went on emergency status and the alert lasted forty-eight hours or more. Then they concluded that the Cheyennes did not plan to attack. The warriors who had gone on the warpath had already left, heading north toward the Powder. The older men and the rest of the tribe remained in their tepees, either in shame at their peaceful decision or for fear that they might be punished for the acts of the hostiles.

There had actually been two separate alarms at the Indian Agency, the second one coming just before dusk this evening. A picket had seen the young Cheyennes coming down from the north, and everyone had jumped to the conclusion that the war party had doubled back to attack Fort Robinson. Defense positions had been manned once more, the state of tension lasting until it was discovered that the apparently menacing Indians were actually refugees themselves. In the gloom of evening the anxious people at the Agency had not seen the Fifth in pursuit of the Cheyennes and they had been on a constant alert until Merritt's staff officer rode up to explain what had happened.

Some of the latter details never came through clearly to Kirby. He had settled back in his blanket after hearing that Nell was safe and that Lowry was in jail. He could understand the anxious moments at the Agency and see how they might have been thrown into a state of alarm at sight of the Cheyennes coming toward them. But he didn't care very much. His eyes were getting mighty heavy.

Then he forced them open as Truitt's voice came through to him more urgently. A few words penetrated the fog of heavy sleep. "Lowry. Mrs. Perry. Don't know wheah . . . Neveh missed until this moahnin' . . ."

Every bone and sinew protested when he moved, but the aches helped to get him awake. It was morning. Truitt was not just still here; he was *back*. Something had happened during the night.

He didn't waste time in getting the story out of the drawling sergeant. Snapping his questions rapidly he drew out the main facts. Lowry had disappeared from the Agency. Nell Perry was also missing. No one had seen them together.

No one had seen either of them leave the place. But Lowry had been released from his cell at the time of the false alarm the evening before. With all of those Cheyennes coming straight toward the Agency it appeared that every man would be needed to bear arms. Lowry could be used in the defense. He had more reason than most of the others to fear Cheyenne treatment, so it had seemed like a smart idea to use him. The trouble was that no one in authority had remembered to lock him up again when the alarm proved to be false. He had apparently taken advantage of the oversight and of the cessation of Indian hostilities to make good his escape. The clear implication was that Nell Perry had gone with him. Whether she had gone willingly or not no one could be quite sure.

Kirby was talking to himself as he prepared to move. This was what happened when he took things for granted. Once more he had been within striking distance of Lowry but he had forgotten the hard learned lesson. Lowry was slippery. He had gotten away at the last minute on other occasions. Kirby blamed himself for assuming that even a military jail would have held the fellow.

Much of the self condemnation was forced, he realized. He wasn't half so angry at Lowry's escape as he was worried at the disappearance of Nell Perry. Somehow Lowry didn't count for so much any more.

CHAPTER 12

There was a message from General Merritt that had been left the night before, but it only repeated the false assurance Truitt had given at that time. Apparently no one at the Agency had been aware that Lowry had made his escape.

"Too much excitement last night," Truitt explained as they went across to the huddle of buildings that served as administrative headquarters for the area. "Fust off they'd been figge'in' that they had a private Injun wah on theah hands. Then one o' theah pet Injuns brung in the tale about the fight on the Little Bigho'n and they got moah sca'ed than evah. Last night they got all spooked up again when it looked like all them Injuns was comin' at 'em. Seems like they didn't have no time to do much thinkin'."

Kirby knew that it explained the error, even though he didn't want to accept any explanation no matter how good it was. The only thing that counted was that Joe Lowry had slipped clear again and this time had done something to Nell Perry so that she had accompanied him. Kirby was still blaming himself for having gone to sleep instead of making some personal investigation. So he could also blame others who had slipped up on their responsibilities. Not that it mattered who was to be blamed; the damage was done. Now something had to be worked out to undo it.

Truitt took him to a clerk named Meadows, a brisk young fellow who seemed to have some authority and who apparently knew a bit about Kirby's interest in Mrs. Perry and Joe Lowry. He also knew that General Merritt had spoken on Kirby's behalf and the fact clearly impressed him. He wanted to be helpful.

"We've tried to run down every clue as to what happened," he told Kirby grimly. "We think Lowry slipped away from here quite early last evening, perhaps while the rest of us were just beginning to celebrate getting over our scare." He grimaced a little as he added, "It looked mighty bad to have all that mob of Indians coming right at us last night. We were some time in finding out that they were fugitives and not attackers. At least it seemed like a long time to us."

"Then you think Lowry ducked out at that point?"

"It seems so. The men who were on the same defensive position recall him being with them while they were watching the approaching Cheyennes. When the Indians turned toward their village and the troops appeared in the distance behind them the excitement broke out here. Nobody remembers seeing Lowry after that moment."

"And Mrs. Perry? Where was she at that time?"

"All women were in the store room. A couple of them recall that Mrs. Perry helped calm the children when we first ran to defense positions. They remember that a man came to the door and called to her, but they didn't see the man. She went out with him."

"Can they fix the time?"

"Close enough. They didn't think to report it because it was right afterwards that they heard the good news. Nobody was in any mood to think about anything but being safe."

"Seems safe to assume that Lowry persuaded her to go with him," Kirby said shortly. "Did she take any baggage?"

"We don't know. She traveled light and she had not been here long enough for anyone to know much about her property. If she took anything with her it wasn't very much. My guess is that she went just as she was."

"By force?"

Meadows seemed a trifle uneasy with this part of his information, but he finally nodded. "We're afraid that's how it happened. We know that two horses are missing from the stables. Also two saddles and other gear. And Lowry was armed. A carbine was issued to him when he was placed on defense duty."

There seemed to be no doubt about what had happened. For Kirby the only question was the matter of Nell's attitude. And he wasn't sure why it made any difference. For her to have gone willingly would have been as bad in many respects as for her to have been dragged along by force. Still he wanted to know.

"Why do you think she went by force?" he asked the clerk. "She was his stepsister, you know, and she came here to find him as a friendly gesture involving some inherited property."

Meadows shrugged. "It's none of my business, mister, but I saw a few things and I heard some talk. I took her to the jail to see him when she first arrived. Before the trouble broke, that was. I heard him whining about being innocent and he sounded completely sickening to me. She told him she was sorry to find him in such a state but that he should not bother to protest his innocence, that she was quite aware that he was a despicable character in a lot of ways.

"Then he dropped his whine and warned her that he'd make her change her tune when he got out of jail. She knew, of course, that he was in there because he preferred jail to having the old Cheyennes lift his hair for what he'd done in stirrin' up the younger braves. So she just laughed at him. Not a happy laugh, you know. Bitter, you could call it."

"But she still went with him when he called her out of the store room during that last alarm?"

"Seems so. We can't find anybody else who'll admit to calling her out. My guess is that Lowry called her and then put a gun on her to make her go with him to the stable . . . and on away from the post."

"Any idea which way they went?"

"We've got a couple of friendly Indians out there checking the sign right now. With troops riding all around the place last night there wouldn't be any decent tracks close to the buildings. Before long we ought to have a hint as to where they went."

"Thanks. I'll be back as soon as I can get ready to ride. If you get information about their tracks, you can pass the word to me at the scout camp. I'll be getting myself some breakfast."

The Agency clerk seemed to think that was an odd remark, but Kirby meant it exactly as he had said it. Within the next few minutes he proposed to get on the trail of Lowry and Nell, whether the Indians found such a trail or not. Making proper preparations would be just as important as a prompt start and a decent meal was one of the preparations he knew ought to be made. Eating had been almost as badly neglected as sleeping during the past few days.

The camp of the Fifth was already bustling with a different kind of preparation when he went back to it. General Merritt had allowed his men a good night of rest, but now he had to get them on the trail again. Their orders still called for them to march in support of General Crook and they were many more miles away from the Bighorns than they had been when the orders were issued. Kirby said his farewells to Cody, Winans, and the others, but Sergeant Truitt stayed with him. Truitt was in the happy position of being forgotten. His own unit was miles away and only Colonel Stanton seemed to have any responsibility for the sergeant or his three men. And Colonel Stanton wasn't paying any attention to them. Apparently the paymaster had forgotten that the quartet had been added to his escort for the purpose of looking after Mrs. Perry. Or perhaps he knew that they had really been sent along to get them away from the ire of Lieutenant Beckwith. One way or another he chose to ignore them.

Kirby recognized the situation enough to make use of it. "Sergeant," he said between swallows of his breakfast. "I want to know all I can about the trails out of here. Find out what new ones have been opened in the years since I worked through the area. I've got a hunch that the way to catch Lowry is to outguess him instead of trail him."

"Any trails in pahticklah yo' want to know about?"

"Ones leading to the railroad. I don't think Lowry will risk his scalp in Cheyenne country, now that he knows the Indians are sore at him. And he won't head for an army post where he might be arrested. We don't have too many choices left. Check into any regular trails leading toward Fort Sedgwick or Julesburg. He has been running liquor into this part of the country, and I don't think it has been coming in from such places as Fort Laramie or Cheyenne. That leaves the rail stations as the best bet."

Truitt hurried away and Kirby was left to think about another problem. Why had Lowry taken Nell with him? Obviously the man's first thought had been a simple escape. He had to get away from the army and he had to make good his escape through the Cheyennes who would be worse than the army as captors. So why should he have burdened himself with a prisoner who could only slow him down? Kirby didn't like any of the answers which came to his mind.

He finished a hasty meal, checked his gear with great care and secured extra ammunition from Bill Cody. The Warbonnet fight had required a lot of shells, and he didn't want to start off on any pursuit of Lowry without knowing that he would be able to defend himself both against the outlaw and against any wandering tribesman who might be encountered.

By the time he had made his preparations Truitt was back, reporting that a number of wagon trails had been opened to the south since the advent of the railroad. In the old days the Agency had been supplied almost entirely from Fort Laramie, but now there were shorter and more convenient lines of supply. There was a trail up from Fort Mitchell which skirted around the western end of the Niobrara hills, a branch of it swinging to the east to hit the Overland Trail northwest of Julesburg. A somewhat less known trail swung east beyond the Niobrara. It was not used by wagons but was believed to have several eastern branches, leading variously to Julesburg, South Platte, or Fort McPherson.

"Any word from the trackers?" Kirby asked.

"Ain't in yet."

Kirby went back to the Agency with him, requesting and receiving an interview with Colonel Stanton. "I'd like to ask a favor, Colonel," he said bluntly.

"Ask away. General Merritt left word that any help we could give you he would appreciate."

"That's fine. You have four men detailed to your party for the purpose of keeping an eye on Mrs. Helen Perry. I think it's reasonable to ask that they be used for the purpose of finding her once more. I don't blame them for her disappearance, you understand. I simply . . ."

"You simply want to borrow them. Fair enough. What do you want them to do?"

"I'd like to put them on the trail of Lowry and Mrs. Perry, when and if the trail is discovered by the Agency trackers. I don't suppose there are men here who can be spared for the job just now, but Sergeant Truitt and his men are not committed to anything."

Colonel Stanton frowned after his first show of good humor. "I don't quite understand. You want these men to accompany you?"

"No. I want them to follow the trail if it's picked up. I've got a feeling that maybe I can take a short cut, if I'm reading Lowry's mind correctly. It could put me close up behind him and pick up some of the time we've lost. But I don't want all my eggs in one basket. If my guess is wrong, I want to know that somebody else is playing it the safer way."

"It sounds all right to me," Stanton told him. "I'll give Sergeant Truitt the order and make it official. Anything else?"

"No, sir. Just lay it on thick when you make your report about sending the message to General Merritt. It would be a hell of a note if he got into a jam over this."

Stanton smiled. "Don't worry about Merritt. You've got problems of your own."

He wasn't just saying it, Kirby thought. The big problem was to outguess a man who had been working this country on the sly for several years and would undoubtedly know trails that were otherwise known only to the Indians. Trying to outsmart him was going to be a real problem.

When he left the Agency, he did not yet know what report the trackers would make. The Indians who had gone out to search for the trail had not even come back. One report said that they had been seen going in the direction of the principal Cheyenne village, but no one seemed to be sure.

Truitt brought his three men over to where Kirby was getting into the saddle. "Better give yoah ohdehs to all of us, Mistah Kuhby," the sergeant suggested. "Ah reckon this is goin' to be the kind o' job wheah ain't nobody goin' to give ohdehs. We got to wo'k togetheh; that's all."

Kirby explained what he had in mind, warning them to take plenty of food and ammunition and to be wary of ambushes, either by Lowry or by renegade Indians. It was the same sort of warning he had been giving himself.

"One thing," one of the troopers cut in. Kirby thought it was the man named Bradway, but he didn't inquire about it. "I got an idea about them trackers goin' toward the Injun camp. I think they hit a trail but they want somebody else to know about it before they report back here."

"These Cheyennes are supposed to be trustworthy," Kirby objected. "At the moment I wouldn't suppose they'd be too welcome in the camp."

"You're forgettin' something, mister," the man replied. "That Injun camp's split wide open. There was a sort of committee of old chiefs out to kill this Lowry polecat long before any of the big fuss started. They blame him for gettin' their sons into trouble. Now I reckon they got more reason to be sore at him. Maybe they've made a move or two toward findin' him."

"Possible," Kirby admitted. "Anyway, you fellows keep it in mind; I'm going to be a long way ahead of the Cheyennes if my guess is right."

He rode out of the Agency without fanfare, anxious not to let any watching Indians know what he was about. It had been all good fun to gloat over the way the Cheyennes had been so thoroughly cowed, but Kirby knew that the tribal attitude might not be the attitude of some isolated individuals. A few braves might try to take out their resentment on any convenient white man. Kirby did not want to be too conspicuous.

He rode hard for a few miles but then slowed the pace as he began to move into the more broken country north of the Niobrara. He crossed the stream without difficulty and found the trail he thought he could remember, following its twisting course to the summit of the wooded hills which flanked the stream on its south side. This was actually the divide which separated the valley of the Platte from the double valley of the Niobrara and South Cheyenne. It was the high country the main trails avoided.

Twice he crossed fairly well-defined hunting trails, but there was no fresh sign on any of them. It was beginning to be pretty certain that he had made one good guess. No matter what anyone else had thought, he did not believe that Lowry would strike out for any settlement. Julesburg or South Platte would be just as dangerous to him as Fort Laramie or Fort Fetterman. The man was up to some kind of trick which would make it worth while for him to have taken Nell Perry along. Kirby didn't yet know what it was, but he had made his opening move with the assumption that Lowry must have some supply line which had run through relatively unknown country. The best bet was that such a line must have come in from the southeast, probably through the desolate sandhill region that stretched for so many miles south of the Black Hills and the Badlands.

He rested at noon, more for the sake of the horse than for himself, going on through the heat of the day in the hope that Lowry's move would have been a slow one. There were several good reasons to have such a hope. Lowry's primary aim would have been to throw off direct pursuit so he would have done some dodging for that purpose. In the second place he had done his traveling at night and in the third place he would be slowed by his prisoner. Kirby wanted to take full advantage of those facts.

Late in the afternoon he began to find more familiar appearing country. This was the hill region he had had in mind. He wasn't sure why he had believed that Lowry would strike for this spot, but it had been not only a good hunch but also a bit of careful reasoning. Now he was beginning to wonder. There had been no sign of life all day, no trails of anyone.

He climbed a rise which permitted him to scan the countryside in all directions and almost immediately spotted dust to the northeast. Riders were working up the valley of a small stream which flowed up from the south into the Niobrara. Because the country was fairly well wooded Kirby knew that there would be no chance for him to see them, or him, if it should be only one. He had to take a look. It wasn't where he expected Lowry to be, but he could not pass up any chances.

A glance at the sun gave him an idea of the amount of daylight that would be left to him, so he decided to cut back toward the Niobrara. He ought to find tracks there which would tell him something. It might save him chasing a couple of Indian hunters who would mean nothing to him. Nothing but trouble, that is. At the same time he might find something in the valley of the river that would help.

He stopped once at a brook which seemed to have a little less alkali in its water than most of them did, filled his canteen, and let his horse drink as much of the bad tasting stuff as he wanted.

On a small rise he saw the dust again, changing his mind about it. The dust makers were really going down the Niobrara, not up another creek as he had first supposed. Unless he was now seeing a different lot of dust. He could not be sure on that point, so he decided that he should make a pretty thorough examination of the river banks. He had to know what was happening.

It took him several minutes to reach the sandy river bank, but, when he looked again toward the east, there was no dust to be seen. This time he felt certain that his angle of sight was such that he should still be able to see the unknown—but he couldn't. A little nearer to him there was a faint haze of dust lingering above the trees, but even that was something he was almost willing to charge off to imagination. Certainly no new dust was rising.

Then he broke off his puzzling to search for signs. He found none. The wide stretch of flatland between the water and the first rise of the hills should have offered plenty of opportunity to find tracks. There simply were no signs here.

The far side didn't appear to be the side riders would have chosen, but Kirby had to have a look. He crossed through the shallow water and searched the north bank with great care. Still no tracks.

Not knowing what else to do he sent his mount downstream, studying the ground as he rode. At the first convenient spot he crossed back to the south bank—and found tracks. Two shod ponies had passed this way not many minutes earlier, heading downstream.

This time he thought he knew what it meant, but he backtracked them to be certain. Scarcely a hundred yards from the spot where he had found them he spotted the place where they had emerged from the stream. A hasty look around showed no evidence that anyone had entered it. These were the tracks of fugitives trying to baffle trackers. And Joe Lowry was the only known fugitive in the region. Joe was forcing Nell to follow his lead, probably carrying out a program of trail blotting that he had started during the night. Sergeant Truitt and his men were going to have a problem of working it out.

There was a certain amount of satisfaction in knowing that he had guessed correctly. He even thought he could estimate where the earlier trail had been. Lowry's trick would have been to pretend that he was heading toward a known town, probably along one of the used trails. Then he would have cut away at a creek crossing, doubling and dodging until he reached a fork of the Niobrara. Now he was still playing tricks to throw off pursuit. Because Kirby had anticipated such a move he had come straight across to the right part of the country, picking up several hours on the fugitives while Lowry played his tricks.

Being a little proud of himself didn't make him forget the dangerous and less satisfying part of this business. He still didn't know why Nell had come along with her stepbrother. Either she was behaving pretty stupidly or she was in trouble. He didn't quite know which he hoped it was.

Actually it wasn't anything for him to worry about just yet. Lowry's trail-blotting tactics would thwart most pursuers. Kirby wouldn't be getting any help for a long time to come—even if the others worked their way through the confused trail. He would have to do the job alone, and it never was an easy task to get a hostage away from a killer who would stop at nothing. But that was the way it had to be. After eight years of tracking this man he was finally about to catch up with him. Himself against Lowry. That was the way it ought to be.

Then he saw new signs along the river bank. Ten unshod ponies had crossed the stream some hours before the other two riders had come along. The exact time interval between the making of the two sets of tracks was not clear, but Kirby didn't like the idea at all. Those Indians might be trailing the other pair right now, watching from the other side of the river.

CHAPTER 13

With darkness not many minutes away he knew that he had to make a decision. He could go on following the trail of the two riders or he could take a detour to find out what these Indians were doing. There simply was not time for him to do both.

He weighed the possibilities in each case and decided to follow the Indian sign, at least far enough to see what direction it would take on the far side of the river. His pursuit of Lowry and Nell Perry would have to wait. He couldn't afford to go blundering in on the trail of his own quarry only to become a possible third victim for a renegade war party.

It did not concern him very much that the Indians had passed this point first. If they had remained close to the river on the far side, they certainly would have seen the other two people. They might even now be swinging back to attack them. That part was the risk he had to take. He didn't want Indians behind him when he made his move.

He crossed at the same ford the warriors had used, a prickly feeling at his scalp as he sent the weary horse splashing across. There was a lot of brush country on the far side, just the right kind of brush to conceal an Indian ambush. It wasn't comfortable to be such an exposed target.

Nothing happened, however, and he picked up the trail at once, finding that it led through the brush of the river bottoms and up into some of that rugged mixture of sandhills, scrub timber, and clay gullies which seemed so common in this part of the territory. As he had feared, the Indian trail began to run parallel to the river, the Indians keeping to cover but in position to watch the stream and its valley.

A quarter of a mile later an extra pony track joined the trail, and he still had light enough to see that some kind of conference had taken place here. The eleventh warrior obviously had been a part of this band.

Suddenly Kirby had an idea. This was beginning to add up to something more than a little awkward. He remembered a number of remarks he had heard at the Agency. The elders of the Cheyenne tribe had been out to get Lowry, blaming him for the debauchery of their young men. Probably they would blame him all the more now that the Warbonnet defeat had been suffered. And there had been a hint that the Agent's trackers had not reported back to him immediately but had gone instead to the Indian village. What more likely than that the Indians wanted first crack at Lowry? Just as Kirby had done, they had come straight to this desolate region, probably knowing that Lowry had some kind of hideout here. They could have made the journey in less time than it had taken Kirby because they would not have needed to grope around.

He could sympathize with them, but he realized that his own safety and that of Nell Perry would be affected. These Indians were bitter; they would not feel kindly disposed toward any white. And they would not want witnesses to what they were undoubtedly planning. Getting Nell away might turn out to be a very risky proposition.

The light failed him before he could work out the trail much farther, so he picked a convenient gulley and worked his way down through it to a spot where brushy growth gave him a degree of concealment for his horse. It was a miserable camp, hot and full of mosquitoes, but he preferred it to the more open country. Tonight open country would not be healthy.

He made a supper out of hard rations and the alkali water which he had been carrying in his canteen until it was almost hot. Then he climbed back to higher ground for a final look around. Darkness was full upon the sandhill country by that time, the last final tints of pink having gone out of the west. Somewhere off to the north thunder grumbled uneasily, but the storm was so far away that no clouds blotted the stars and only twice did he spot the faint glare of the lightning. Under other circumstances he might have thought of it as a fine July evening, but now he had no ideas about appreciating nature. There were too many other things to be considered, none of them pleasant.

Then he saw something else. At first it appeared to be a star close to the eastern horizon, but as he moved it disappeared and then brightened. A camp fire. And on the north side of the river. Apparently the Indians had not been too far ahead of them when they had halted for the night.

His first thought was to get his horse and move back to the other side of the river, seeking somewhat safer areas. Then he changed his mind. In this business he couldn't afford to be playing it safe. The bold course was the one to take. Perhaps he could get close enough to the Indian camp to get some kind of line on them. Maybe he could even get them to accept him in peace. Perhaps he could make a deal with them; let them go after Lowry but permit him to go along for the protection and rescue of Nell Perry.

It didn't seem to make much sense even as he thought of it, but he knew that he had to do some gambling. These Indians had played a pretty decent role thus far. At least they had if they were the old chiefs he had guessed them to be. It just might work.

He marked his camp site carefully so he would be able to find it again in the darkness. Then he unbuckled his gun belt and left it with his saddle, taking with him only his six-gun. No extra cartridges or anything else metallic to make a jingle that might betray him. Tonight he was going to play Indian well enough to fool Indians. He had to do it right.

Even with that distant fire as a beacon he found the going difficult. This was rugged country in daylight; at night it was almost impossible. He stumbled into gullies and climbed out again. He became tangled in brush. He had to make long detours around other dry washes too steep to go through. And always he had to move with the idea in mind that the Indians might have sentinels out who would hear his scramblings.

It seemed to him that he had taken hours for the approach, but, when he caught his first glimpse of the Indian camp, he saw that the warriors there were just finishing their evening meal. He counted them and found to his surprise and satisfaction that there were eleven of them. Unless they had picked up additional numbers since he had last seen their tracks, there were no pickets out. Probably they didn't believe that anyone else was near.

They had made camp on a bit of flat ground between two gullies, the brush along each dry wash helping to screen them. Only a break toward the south had permitted Kirby to spot the fire in the first place. At once he saw his chance. If he could get into that near wash without knocking a lot of loose stone around, he could creep within a few yards of the camp, lying concealed in the gulley while he tried to figure out what they were planning to do.

It took time. He had to find a spot where he could get down into the arroyo without starting a sand slide and then he had to crawl toward the Indians, making sure that he tested every square inch of ground for loose stones before putting a hand or knee on it. He used up a good twenty minutes in covering the hundred-foot distance, but finally he was able to find a spot where the bank sloped up gently to a clump of bushes. There he could lie flat and peer beneath the branches in almost perfect concealment and some degree of comfort. He had already tied his bandana across the lower part of his face as a precaution against getting alkali dust in his nostrils. A sneeze at this juncture might prove fatal.

Almost as soon as he began to study the group at the dying fire, he realized that he was looking at a pretty unique scene, perhaps a scene which no white man had ever witnessed and lived to report. These Indians were in solemn conference as a court. The typically Indian ceremonies had obviously begun while he was still crawling through the gulley, but the general routine was familiar enough. The lengthy preliminaries went with every formal move made by the Indians. What caught real attention was the course these ceremonies were taking. Allowing for the difference in language and setting this had all the marks of a vigilantes' meeting.

Kirby's knowledge of the Cheyenne tongue was not thorough enough for him to understand every word or even to get the exact meaning in every statement, but the general tenor of the meeting was completely clear. His guess had been correct. These Indians were a sort of extermination committee dedicated to the proposition that one Joe Lowry had to die. White man's law had not punished him, so the elders of the Cheyennes would accomplish that worthy purpose.

Kirby found himself almost nodding agreement. What they were saying about Lowry suited him exactly. He could have added a few more indictments to the list they were compiling, and it seemed oddly improper that he should not be taking some part in this meeting. He really had a claim to be some sort of senior partner in the undertaking.

As he listened he heard a few names, but none of them were familiar to him. He decided that none of these men were important chiefs. These were elderly warriors or minor chiefs who had undertaken what they clearly felt to be an obligation to their people. Kirby could not see well enough in the dim firelight to judge ages, but the voices told him something. He estimated that only one of the Indians was as young as thirty, the other ten quite elderly. He guessed that the young one might be the son of these elders.

Then he caught a name which brought recognition. Yellow Hand. That had been the name of the young chief Bill Cody had killed and scalped in the Warbonnet fight. What did Yellow Hand have to do with this?

Again his knowledge of the Cheyenne tongue made it difficult for him to translate some of the more rhetorical forms of Indian speech, but gradually the idea began to get through. Yellow Hand had been one of Lowry's principal customers. Yellow Hand had raised hell because he was often full of bad whiskey. Yellow Hand's death was a sort of symbol of bad judgment and ignominious defeat. Yellow Hand's father had required the scalp of the whiskey peddler, his son having lost his scalp because of dealings with the great enemy of the Cheyenne people.

There was something of an argument then but Kirby could follow it well enough. Each member of the council seemed to repeat some statement or other, and the repetition helped the listener to get his translation straight. They were actually voting, each man stating his belief, either that he was willing to take Lowry's scalp back to the father of the dead Yellow Hand or that he did not think this should be a matter of personal feeling, that Lowry's death was for the tribe and not for one family. The younger warrior, who spoke last, stated that he was opposed to taking any white man's scalp back to the reservation at a time like this. There had been enough trouble without risking more.

The vote seemed to favor the claim of Yellow Hand's father—or whatever relative he was. Kirby could not be certain. What was definite was that these old men were disposing of the scalp as though they already had it in their possession. Obviously they were pretty sure of catching Lowry.

Meanwhile the listener had been able to pick up various other bits of information to let him understand the rest of the story. Again he could fit their remarks into previous information. The Indian Police at the Agency had indeed reported to the tribe before going back to tell the Agent what they had seen in their search for Lowry's sign. Immediately the vigilantes—as Kirby was mentally naming them by this time—had started out on their mission, half of them aiming straight for this part of the country because they knew that Lowry and another unnamed man had maintained a liquor cache somewhere nearby. Others had fanned out to make sure that they were not being fooled and that Lowry was not actually going in some other direction. They must have assured themselves on the score quite promptly for they had reassembled rapidly even before Kirby could reach the same spot. His fumbling attempts to remember the terrain had put him just behind them, although he had been working on the same guess—that Lowry would be moving into this broken land of gullies and brushy hills.

It occurred to him that he had been lucky that his own route had been a little longer. If he had arrived ahead of the Indians, they would have seen his sign instead of his being able to see theirs. Now it seemed obvious that they expected no white man to appear in the region before at least another day. They were making plans with that specifically in mind. They expected to catch Lowry late in the morning of the next day.

Kirby knew that he was hearing the talk of old men. These were not the kind of warriors who preferred the slashing dawn attack. They knew that Lowry would be holed up at the cache they had mentioned so often in their talk. There would be no hurry. He could have the morning to relax his vigilance and then they would take him. Even old men could approach the hidden spot quite easily.

Kirby was certain that they used language that inferred capturing rather than killing him. Along with the vote over the disposal of his scalp the inference was clear. Lowry was not to die easily. Again Kirby found himself grimly in accord with these red vigilantes. Whatever happened to Joe Lowry would be too good for him. What really mattered now was that the Indians had never once referred to Lowry's having a companion. There had been mention of a partner in the whiskey business, but Kirby understood that the partner had already fallen victim to this same board of executioners. Why didn't the Cheyennes speak of Nell Perry? Certainly they knew that their intended victim had taken the woman with him when he escaped from the Agency. Certainly they had seen the double set of hoofprints.

Suddenly Kirby had a sick feeling. He had seen two sets of prints, but he had no way of knowing that Nell was on one of those ponies. Was it possible that Lowry had killed his stepsister and was simply taking a riderless horse along with him? For an instant Kirby thought of slipping away and hitting the Lowry back trail at once. The Indians would take care of Lowry, he felt sure; maybe he could find Nell before it was too late.

Then reason returned. Those pony tracks had never been in tandem except in the narrow places. One pony had followed the other as though on a lead rope going into the river or coming out. Otherwise the tracks had been side by side. There must have been a rider on the second horse.

He settled down to listen once more and immediately heard mention of Nell. The Cheyennes had discussed what they evidently considered to be the more important aspects of their business and now they would talk about the squaw who had come into the picture. They evidently considered the woman as a prisoner, but there was a sharp difference of opinion as to what should be done about her. Some of the older men, the ones whose talk had sounded most peaceful, wanted to return her to the Agency as a sign of their good will. They were outvoted, however, by the others. No matter what Joe Lowry had done, he was still a white man and the times were bad. Any Indian who killed a white man now would be in trouble. There must be no witness to this execution.

Kirby knew what he had to do then. He had to get Lowry first. And he had to get himself and Nell away before the Cheyennes could move in. They would probably be just as angry at him for cheating them out of their vengeance as they would have been if he had actually tried to help Lowry.

The thought brought with it another kind of realization. A month ago he would have felt just as angry if someone else had gotten to Lowry ahead of him. He had been thinking then just as these Indians were thinking now. He was not quite sure when or how he had changed his attitude, but he knew that he had changed it. Lowry had become just a source of trouble and danger. It did not make too much difference whether the eight-year vengeance trail should come to an interrupted conclusion.

He crawled away as silently as he had

approached, using the same kind of caution as before but with his mind racing ahead of his slow progress. He had to make his move and he had to make it tonight, taking advantage of the fact that the Indians behind him were old men. They would rest long after the hard day's ride. They were remorseless but in no hurry. Kirby had to be in a hurry. It could make the difference.

The worst part was that he did not know exactly where to find Lowry. The Cheyennes had spoken only generally of the place, referring to it merely in their time calculations for the morrow. An hour's ride, they had called it. And they had twice referred to the spot as being well hidden but also easy of approach because of the brush surrounding it. They would cross the river near their present camp and approach from the hills. That much Kirby understood; the rest he had to guess.

It took what seemed like a terrifically long time for him to find his own hidden camp and by that time he didn't dare to try for some needed sleep. He wanted to be across the river before the moon rose, and he realized that he had completely lost track of such matters as moon schedules. He wasn't sure how many days had passed since he had figured moonrise as an hour or two before midnight, but he guessed that there would be several hours of moonlight before the dawn. He wanted to be well away from the Indian camp before any such light could appear. It was just possible that the old chiefs would have a sentry or two on duty in the latter part of the night. He couldn't afford to be detected, particularly when he had the problem of crossing a strange river in the dark.

He led his horse all the way, keeping to one of the dry washes which led to the shallow stream and then groping a precarious way across. Once he had to back out of what seemed dangerously like a patch of quicksand, but, after a bit of wallowing around, he found harder bottom and presently was able to clamber out on the far shore. He had a wry moment of satisfaction in the thought that no storm had hit the region to cause high water. With so much crossing and recrossing of the Niobrara he would have had a lot more trouble if the river hadn't been at such a low level.

Almost unconsciously he turned to scan the starry horizons, wondering whether he might not hope for some freak storm to swell the river and delay those grim Cheyennes. Then he shrugged off the thought. The night was cloudless. And anyway summer storms usually didn't come up in the late hours. Once the afternoon and evening had passed there was usually little chance of rain. He was on his own. Whatever he might manage to accomplish would have to be done without help from nature.

CHAPTER 14

Now a different kind of decision had to be made. He must find Lowry's hideout and still leave no trail which the Cheyennes could find. His only advantage was that no one knew of his presence on the scene. He had to preserve that advantage if he could possibly manage it.

Travel along the river bank would mean that his track would be spotted by the Cheyennes when they made their crossing. If he tried to make a detour back into the hills, he would be taking an even greater risk of trouble. The Indians proposed to make such a detour, and Kirby could not even guess how they would do it. If he didn't cut far enough away from the river they might still pick up his sign. If he cut too far he might lose his objective entirely and at best he would lose a lot of valuable time. Time was getting to be mighty important.

There had been a clear hint that Lowry's hideout was fairly close to the river. Evidently it could be located somewhat more readily from that angle. For Kirby there seemed to be only one gamble that was worth taking. He had to use the same strategy that Lowry had used on the previous day. Let the river cover his tracks.

He rode downstream a few hundred yards,

making his first gamble on a guess at where the Cheyennes would cross. He assumed that they would ford the river fairly close to their present camp but not upstream from it. So he kept to the river bank until he reached what he considered to be the danger area, then sent the pony into the water.

It was slow, treacherous travel but he let the horse pick the way, alternately floundering through deep holes and scrambling through shallows. Once the pony came out on a bare sand bar and Kirby had to dismount and do some careful trail blotting in the darkness. He was wet and muddy when he completed the job but that was not important. He had been wet and muddy ever since that first crossing. What counted most was that he had washed away the prints which might have been noticed from the river bank.

He kept to the water for what he believed to be a good mile and by that time the crescent moon was showing in the east, outlining hills and brushy clumps to tell him that this was still the kind of country he had traversed on the previous afternoon. It also warned him that the night was wearing thin. He had to get out on the bank and hope that the Indians would have made their proposed cut into the hills instead of coming this far down the river.

Also he had to make his guess as to what the Cheyennes had meant in referring to an hour's ride. After all, an hour was a white man's unit of time. When an Indian spoke of an hour what did he mean?

The only reasonable guess was that these reservation Indians had become accustomed to the white man's clock. They meant what anyone else would mean or they would not have used the term. An hour was an hour. But did they mean an hour of direct travel or an hour by the indirect route they were planning to use? And how would that have to be adjusted for Kirby's slow progress? It would be pretty difficult to guess what time should have elapsed for a normal trip across the country he had just struggled through.

He decided to forget the calculations and concentrate on finding a brush-screened gulley which might fit the description he had overheard. It ought to be a dry wash which came into the Niobrara from the south. Hence it should be most easily located from the river itself.

Ten minutes later he struck a sandy area along the river. Dismounting he examined the ground in the faint moonlight. The tracks were there. He read the sign as much by feel as by sight, but he was sure of it. Two riders had passed this spot recently enough so that the sign was clear and distinct. At least he could move ahead with the knowledge that he had not already passed the turn-off.

There was no hope of doing any kind of

tracking job so he rode on once more, watching now for terrain such as the Cheyennes had mentioned. A mile dropped behind him. Then another. The moon was fading out a little now, and he could sense rather than see a lightening of the eastern sky. Dawn would be coming over the hills quickly now, and he could hope for a bit of sign reading that would take him to the people he sought.

Here and there a bird began to chirp restlessly in the brush, their notes beginning that subtle change which turns night sounds into day sounds. He wondered why it was that no one ever seemed to hear that constant insect drone during the daylight hours. Perhaps the insects shut up as a safety precaution when the birds began to stir around. It seemed like a silly thing to occupy his mind at such a time, but he was content to have it so. Rather such thoughts than the other one which had been nagging for recognition ever since leaving Fort Robinson. He didn't want to let himself think about what might have happened to Nell Perry.

He struck higher ground then, the river valley becoming narrower and deeper as the stream cut its way through a chain of low hills. Then a ravine blocked his climb, and he knew at once that this was the place he was searching for. A creek came up out of the south, cutting itself a passage to the river. Even in the dim light he could see that it came out of a sizeable patch of timber, its lower reaches fringed with bushes and stunted cedars. Lowry had picked a good hideout.

Dawn was bringing out details now and Kirby had no trouble in finding the track of the two horses. He followed the signs as carefully as possible, hopeful of saving valuable minutes. Even elderly Cheyennes would not linger too long on an errand like the present one.

He halted in a patch of timber, removing the shells from his six-gun and working the bullets out with teeth and jackknife. Then he dumped the powder and put them back together again, reloading the gun with harmless cartridges. It was a desperate sort of plan he had in mind, but he could not think of a better one. There would be no opportunity for any real stalking of the man he had sworn to kill. All that mattered now was to get Nell away before the Cheyennes could make their move. He had to ride right in and gamble on the longest kind of odds. If Lowry didn't kill him on sight, he might find a way to get out of the trap. Later he could take whatever other measures seemed possible. In military language he was taking a calculated risk.

The trail became impossible to follow through the thicket, so he simply remained within sight of the creek. He lost the sign and picked it up again twice, not caring now whether he should lose it entirely. From here on he had to look for the kind of cover which could conceal a building of some sort.

The creek took a sharp bend around a steep hill and Kirby moved in close to look down. This was a suitable place, not likely to be seen by a casual passer-by. Not too far from the river but far enough. It was just the kind of location he would have selected if he had been in Lowry's place. A man might pass by without ever looking down into that hollow.

A few seconds later he saw it. Almost hidden behind a screen of cedars and a little lower than where he had halted his horse was a crude little cabin whose green logs had warped and cracked badly. It was really little more than an enclosed shed, but it would have served Lowry's purpose well enough. Almost as he pulled up he heard a horse snort uneasily in the timber a few yards above. This was it. Even though he could still see no sign of human occupancy he did not doubt his hunch. This was it.

Then a harsh rasping voice ordered, "Lift them hands up real high, mister. Fast now!"

Kirby obeyed without turning to look for the speaker. This was it, all right, uncomfortably it. He tried to keep the sudden dismay out of his own tones as he called, "Don't get crazy ideas there. I'm trying to warn you."

The laugh was as unpleasant as the speaking voice. "I'm warned, mister. Warned enough so that I ain't goin' to let you stir outa my gun sights. If you want a slug in your belly just make a wrong move." As he spoke he pushed into sight through the cedars, a carbine aimed steadily at Kirby's middle.

Kirby recalled the long memorized description. The height and build were right. The reddish hair showed beneath the battered hat. Even the missing teeth made a conspicuous hole when the malicious grin parted the thick lips with their week's growth of stubble.

"You Joe Lowry?" Kirby asked.

"You know it. Why are you askin'?"

"I just wanted to make sure that you're the man who needs the warning. It's Lowry the Cheyennes are after."

That shook him up for an instant. The grin disappeared, but the carbine only wavered for a split second. Then the voice snarled, "What Cheyennes?"

Kirby shook his head. "I can't give you names, but last night I slipped close to a Cheyenne camp and heard some mighty odd talk. Ten old bucks and a younger one seemed to be blaming a Joe Lowry for every bad thing that has happened to the tribe since Sand Creek and the Washita. Today they plan to collect your scalp."

"You're a liar. No damned Cheyenne knows how to find me."

"I found you. How do you think I got the

information? You know I didn't follow any tracks during the night."

When Lowry made no reply, Kirby went on quickly, knowing that he had to convince his man or die. "I heard them planning, talking about how they would close in on this spot. Sounded like they'd been here before to kill somebody else they hated almost as much as you."

Lowry swallowed hard but his voice was different as he asked, "Who're you?"

"What does it matter? Get ready to clear out of here while you can still take your hair with you. And stop pointing that damned gun at me! I'm in as much trouble as you are."

Lowry backed up a little but did not lower the carbine. "Get down offa that bronc! . . . Wait. Unbuckle yore gun belt first. Easy. Now let her drop. Stay clear of it when you light down. I've got a real itchy trigger finger."

Kirby swallowed the bitter words which came to him. Lowry's itchy trigger finger was a matter of record. A prospective bride had died because of it.

He was careful to make no sudden move and Lowry circled to get more directly behind him. Then the next order came. "Move down toward that shack. As long as you're tryin' to be such a goddam helpful cuss, I got another job for you. Don't try any tricks!"

Kirby followed orders, knowing that the next

few minutes would be the most dangerous of all. If Lowry had learned of the long pursuit—and it seemed likely that Nell might have told him—he would not hesitate to kill the man who had trailed him for so long. Kirby had to hope that Lowry either did not know or would not guess that this was Mason Kirby under his gun sights now. It would mean a tense moment or two at the shack. He had to be sure that Nell didn't give him away—and he had to keep a strong rein on his self-control so that he didn't betray himself. Anything else would be virtual suicide.

There was more than a little bitterness in realizing how differently he had planned this moment. He had worked out dozens of imaginary scenes where he finally caught up with Joe Lowry, none of them involving any situation like this one. He was on the wrong end of the gun. Still he did not regret the decision that had put him in so much danger. There had not been time to make the kind of search that would have been necessary to locate a well-hidden shack without being observed by a watchful fugitive. The Cheyennes would have come upon the scene long before he could have found the place. He had moved in directly, well aware of the risk he had taken. Now he had to play it Lowry's way until they were out of the hills. After that . . . He wouldn't let himself recognize the all too evident possibility that Lowry would never let him get out of the hills.

His captor was about six feet behind him when he reached the shack, close enough so that he couldn't miss but too far for any attempt to surprise him with a quick attack.

"Open that door!" Lowry ordered, his voice rising slightly in pitch.

Kirby noted the change and knew the danger in it. The man was getting himself worked up for something. The voice which had carried all the pleasing qualities of a hand saw striking a hidden nail now made Kirby think of the same saw being applied to the ragged edge of a tin can. At any moment Joe Lowry might commit another murder.

Kirby tried to divert him. "You picked a good spot for a liquor cache," he observed in as calm a voice as he could muster. "But you can't keep Indians from finding out about places like this. They're sharp, all right."

"Open the door!" Lowry repeated impatiently. "Then go in and untie the woman."

It was Kirby's first real hint that Nell was actually there. Somehow he liked the idea that she had been tied up. At least she had not come with Lowry willingly.

For a moment he had hopes of turning on his man at the doorway and getting him off guard, but then he abandoned the idea. Nell was lying on the dirt floor of the shack, directly in front of the opening. Even a wild shot might strike her. Anyway Lowry had held back just far enough so that he was not open to an attack. He could control both of his prisoners and still not be vulnerable. Even an attempt to slam the door on him wouldn't make much sense. Being trapped weaponless in this shack would be foolhardy. Especially with some very grim old Cheyennes about due to make an appearance.

In the split second which it took for Kirby to think things through he also realized that he had to make sure that Nell didn't betray him. He went forward quickly, hopeful that with the light behind him she would not recognize him until he could make her understand. "Take it easy, lady," he greeted. "I don't know what call this gent's got to have you hawg-tied but he's willin' to let you go now. Roll over a mite and let me get at the ropes."

For an instant there was something like panic in her eyes, and he was afraid she would blurt out his name. Then she swallowed a kind of sob and rolled over obediently.

He untied the combination of cords and scarf which had bound her hands behind her, noticing that the thongs had been pulled brutally tight, but that not much chafing or swelling had resulted. Probably she had not been tied up until after the long ride from Fort Robinson. There would have been no particular reason for such a precaution until night. Then Lowry must have tried to play it safe while he got some sleep. The bruise on her cheek and the tumble of pale hair also suggested that she had not submitted without a struggle. Kirby tried to keep from thinking about it; he didn't dare let himself become angry.

When her hands were free, she struggled to a sitting position, rubbing her wrists gingerly before pushing her hair out of her face. "Thank you, mister," she murmured, not looking up.

"Now ain't that polite!" Lowry jeered. "We're gettin' along real purty, ain't we? Come on, git up! We got to get movin'."

He stepped back a pace, watching them closely and motioning with the carbine. "Get over toward them hosses, both of you."

Kirby stood aside for Nell to go first, hoping that Lowry would let his attention be distracted for one small moment. The man was too smart for that, however, and presently he was walking behind the staggering woman, moving up the slope toward the spot where he had left his horse and gun belt. For a few moments he was sorry he had tried that trick with the cartridges. Maybe Lowry had forgotten the belt.

There was no time for regrets. Lowry wasn't forgetting anything. He halted them at the top of the slope and went carefully around to pick up the belt. Kirby almost made up his mind to risk jumping the man when he passed, but Lowry didn't get close enough. He kept his distance, sidling past while he kept the carbine cocked and aimed. When he stooped to pick up the gun belt he was much too far away for any kind of attack to have a chance.

"Get her into that saddle," he growled at Kirby, motioning first toward Nell and then at Kirby's horse.

Again there was nothing to do but obey. Kirby managed a warning whisper as he lifted Nell to the horse's back, turning it into an audible growl about this being a hell of a way to treat a man who'd gone out of his way to pass a friendly warning.

"That's too damned bad!" Lowry snapped, one of those wolfish grins displaying the missing teeth. "Stop bellyachin' and get over this way before I decide I don't need you no more. Saddle up them other two broncs." He added a grim warning to Nell. "Sit tight where you're at. I'll shoot in one hell of a hurry if you try to bust loose."

"You've got what you want," she told him with a flash of spirit. "Why don't you let me go?"

"Same reason I'm holdin' this pilgrim who got nosy," he told her. "I might have some use for you before this is over. Could be that a Cheyenne might be so interested in a purty yaller scalp that he'd forget about mine for a few minutes."

She bit her lip and made no reply. Kirby kept his back turned, again forcing himself to remember that he wasn't supposed to have any personal interest in either of them.

There was no further talk until Lowry had gotten his prisoners where he wanted them, Kirby directly in front of him and busy with the work of saddling the two horses, Nell sitting Kirby's pony a little to one side. Then Lowry growled, "Let's have that yarn of yours again, mister. How did you say the redskins planned to attack?"

Kirby gave him the full and truthful account, partly because nothing better suggested itself and partly because he wanted Nell to hear it. "I'd say we've got less than an hour to get clear. Maybe less, depending on how long they'll take to get us surrounded. The way I heard it they wanted to be ready to close in shortly before noon. I'd guess they would want plenty of time to do it Indian style."

"You sure you didn't dream all this up?" Lowry demanded.

Kirby glanced over his shoulder as he tightened a cinch. "Wait around and see, if you don't believe me. Right now I'd just as soon take my Cheyenne risks as I would to get shoved around the way you're doing it. Sounded to me like they wasn't mad at anybody but you."

"You ain't got no choice, mister," Lowry sneered. "I'm takin' you along with me till I see can I make some use outa you." He was backing up as he spoke, putting extra distance between himself and Kirby. When he was far enough away to suit him, he cradled the carbine under one arm and buckled the gun belt around his waist. Then he issued a fresh order. "Get on that near hoss and ease over by the lady."

Kirby waited breathlessly to see whether he might exchange the carbine for the six-gun, but Lowry seemed to prefer the weapon he had been carrying. He glanced at the cylinder of the Colt but then thrust it back into the holster. "Get on that hoss!" he repeated impatiently, the carbine swinging up once more. "Try to slow me down, mister, and I might decide that I can git along real good without you!"

CHAPTER 15

Kirby mounted and pulled aside at his captor's order. Then Lowry made a cautious job of getting on the other horse, moving awkwardly as he kept the carbine ready for action. It was becoming pretty clear that he was worried. Those Cheyennes on his trail had good reason to be pretty sore at him and he could not quite make up his mind what he ought to do. He sat in the saddle for a full minute before he asked, somewhat less belligerently, "Which way do you figure we ought to ride?"

Kirby shrugged. He wasn't any happier than Lowry about it. His long shot hadn't paid off, and now it appeared that he was going to be driven right into the muzzles of Cheyenne guns while Lowry held another gun at his back. And he was going to be taking Nell right along with him into deadly peril.

"Say somethin', damn you!" Lowry raged. "You heard them plannin'. Which way could we have the best chance o' breakin' through?"

Again Kirby fell back on a straight answer. Temporarily his own chances were exactly those of Lowry. There was a small chance that the Indian who saw them first might recognize Lowry and make him his target, but that wasn't too much to cheer about. There were too many

Indians. "I'd say we ought to head right straight back the way you came."

"Yeah?" The sneer was back in the rasping voice again. "Want me to dodge Injuns and run smack into some sojers, do you? I ain't that stupid!"

"Figure it out. These Cheyennes are mostly old men. They've already had a day of hard riding. When they start their encircling moves, you know good and well that their best warriors will make the longest circle. They won't expect you to double back, so they'll put their oldest men at that point."

Lowry nodded grudging approval of that reasoning. "Mebbe you're right, at that. Likely to be only one of 'em there."

"That's the way I figured. Now get smart and let me have a gun. With two of us to his one we ought to get past him all right."

"Start ridin'," Lowry ordered. "You ain't gittin' no gun if'n half the Cheyenne tribe is waitin' there!"

He herded them down toward the river, keeping close in their rear with the carbine across the saddle in front of him. Kirby glanced sideways at Nell and commented sourly, "I don't know how you got into this mess, lady, but I sure as hell made a mistake when I tried to help a stranger with a friendly warning. He's usin' us for a shield now."

"Shut up!" Lowry growled. "I'm tryin' to listen fer Injuns."

Nell paid no attention. She returned Kirby's glance and said meaningly, "I'm sorry either one of us ever heard of him." The glance told him a great deal more than she dared to put into words.

"Shut up!" Lowry snarled again.

They rode in silence, all of them listening now for the trouble that was certain to come. Kirby had already heard what sounded like coyotes in the hills but which almost certainly were the signals of the various warriors taking their assigned posts for the attack. There had been no such signal from their immediate front, so he began to hope that he had been right in picking the back trail as the most likely escape route. Still he knew better than to underestimate the wiliness of such a band of experienced warriors. Somewhere directly ahead of them would be a grim old chief who could mean death to all of them.

"Hit the ground at the first sign of trouble," he advised Nell in a low voice. "Don't jump; just fall right off the horse."

"Stop the gab," Lowry snarled.

"Don't talk so big," Kirby retorted over his shoulder. "You don't dare shoot now; you'd give yourself away to the Cheyennes."

"Keep talkin', mister, and you'll find out!"

"Quiet," Nell cautioned.

They had almost reached the river bank. This would be the danger zone, the stretch where death might lurk in any of the numerous brushy patches or cottonwood clumps. Kirby shut his lips tight, keen eyes scanning every suspicious bit of cover.

He tried to put himself mentally in the place of the old warrior who had been left to guard this area. Probably the Indian would resent this post of small honor and would be moving in a little more eagerly than the others, anxious to prove that he was still a great brave. Hurt pride might also dictate that he should try to count coup alone rather than to shout the alarm. Kirby could only hope that the old man would have good eyesight and would recognize Lowry as the proper target for his first ambush shot.

They made their turn to follow the stream westward and then Kirby saw what he had been looking for. A tiny flicker of movement just beyond a thicket of willows about a hundred feet ahead and just beside the trail they were taking.

"Get ready," he warned Nell in an undertone.

Out of the corner of his eye he saw that she was shifting her weight on the saddle. He freed a foot from his stirrup and stared straight at the willows. An ugly black spot was showing there now. It had to be the muzzle of a gun. He saw it move slightly and then steady into position.

"Jump!" he barked suddenly. "Now!" At the

same moment he threw himself from his horse, rolling hard for the protection of the nearest brush.

He heard Lowry's alarmed curse and the crack of a rifle just ahead. His horse shied toward him and he spent seconds getting clear of the clattering hoofs. While he was doing it, there was another gunshot, this one from close at hand. Lowry had fired the carbine.

"Got the bastard!" the grating voice exulted. "The damned fool showed hisself too soon."

Then Kirby had him by the leg, dragging him from his saddle. Lowry cursed again and kicked loose, pulling the six-gun as he rolled clear. Kirby went after him in a headlong dive as the gun came up and emitted a sort of discouraged "sputt!" Before the prone man could pull the trigger a second time, Kirby had him by the throat, using an elbow to keep Lowry from hammering the gun into his face. There was a savage exhilaration in the feel of that whiskery neck between his fingers. After nearly nine years of wishing for it the moment had finally arrived. He clamped down savagely, oblivious to the kicking and threshing that was Lowry's attempt to fight him off.

"Stop it!" Nell exclaimed, limping across toward them. "Mase!! Don't do it. Even now I don't want you to do it!"

Kirby sensed something like hysteria in her

voice. "He's got it coming to him!" he grunted, still squeezing.

"I don't care about him. I don't want you to be a killer. Let him go!"

Something seemed to lift from him then. He still kept his grip on his enemy's throat, but he wasn't trying to tear it in half any longer. "Get his gun belt off," he ordered. "I'll let him up when he can't do any more damage."

She fumbled frantically to remove the belt, Lowry's struggles having subsided enough so that she could accomplish the task. Kirby let the man have a little air but then he clamped down again, still taking a savage joy out of inflicting the punishment. He knew now that he would not kill the miserable creature, but he certainly wasn't going to waste any pity on him.

"Get the six-gun!" he ordered next. "Punch out the shells that are in it and reload with good ones from the belt."

"Very well. But don't kill him."

"Don't worry. I just want to let him have a taste of the hanging he has avoided for so long." He squeezed a little harder and the other man's threshing seemed to subside. Again he let his victim have a small breath but then tightened his grip. Lowry wasn't going to be in any condition to interfere with them when he was finished!

"I'm finished," Nell panted hastily. She shoved the reloaded Colt toward him. "Is he dead?"

"Not quite." He stood up, staring down at his old enemy for a moment before turning to pick up the belt and buckle it on. Then he took the gun from Nell and holstered it. "Pick up the carbine," he told her. "I'll catch that nearest pony. We've got to make some fast tracks out of here."

The horse Nell had been riding had not stampeded with the others, and it took only a few seconds to catch him and mount up. The other two horses had run so far ahead that there would not be time to catch them, so Kirby wheeled to pick Nell up bodily and swing her to the saddle in front of him.

A strangled croak sounded from the ground behind them as the pony went into a run upstream, past a clump of willows where an old Cheyenne chief sagged in death.

"You're going to leave him?" Nell asked, her voice showing the strain.

"Why not? We can't take him with us and anyway we've got plenty of trouble ahead of us without taking any more along."

"But the Indians . . ."

"Can have him." He was curt as he interrupted her. "Hang on tight; I've only got one stirrup." He hadn't noticed when he had saddled the two horses but evidently Nell had been riding side saddle with a regular rig, one stirrup tied up out of the way. He realized that it must have been a pretty uncomfortable business for her. She had covered a lot of miles since leaving the Indian Agency, riding a saddle that had not been built for that kind of work.

He abandoned the thought as a gunshot sounded from the slopes behind them, the slug whining far to the rear but still close enough to be heard. Several Cheyennes were now raising the alarm and Nell made no further suggestions about taking Lowry along. She was too much occupied in trying to hold on, and Kirby was entirely too busy to appreciate the way her arms were clasped around his neck. With only one stirrup and the girl in his arms he did not dare force the pace even though the yelling behind them made him want to do so. There was going to be pursuit; it was important to get as long a lead as possible while the Cheyennes were gathering their wits and forces together.

Just beyond one of the ridges cut by the river they saw a horse ahead. It was Kirby's mount and catching him proved to be fairly simple. They pulled up so that Kirby could reach and grab the reins, then came to a complete halt.

"We've got time to get fixed for a hard run," Kirby said briefly as he dropped Nell to the ground and handed her the reins of the horse they had been riding. "Might as well get straightened out right now. And throw that carbine in the river; we've got no shells for it."

He looked to his own rig and then handed

Nell the other set of reins. "You'd better ride clothespin style now," he said quietly. "It won't look so ladylike, but it'll be a lot better for hard riding. When you're trying to out-run bullets, you can't take time to think about your dignity."

"Dignity!" she exclaimed with a little groan. "I can't even remember what it means. Not after what I've been through lately."

"Cheer up," he advised her. "There's more of the same to come."

"Brute."

"Sorry, Nell," he said in an altered tone. "I guess I must be almost as beat as you are but we've got to keep going. Now climb up there and make yourself as comfortable as possible while I adjust the stirrups to the proper length for you."

She scrambled to the horse's back, trying to tuck her skirts around her thighs to give some protection. "Don't be too particular about comfort," she said resignedly. "There won't be any. I'm already bruised all over."

He grinned up at her. "Why worry so long as it doesn't show."

"Stop talking like an idiot."

"Don't be impolite. Remember you're a lady."

"Of course!" She was heavily sarcastic with the retort. "I'm sure I must look like one."

"You look real good to me. How's that for length?" In spite of his haste he knew that the picture she made was not such an unpleasant one. Her face was dirty and scratched, its bruise beginning to show signs of swelling. Her light summer frock was torn by the brambles, dust stains making its original color somewhat doubtful. But the loose waves of blonde hair rippled in the sun and the shapely leg so close to Kirby's face wore a white stocking that had miraculously remained clean and neat.

"That will do very well," she said primly. "Now, if you've finished staring at me, I think we'd better hurry along. Those yells back there sound closer."

He climbed painfully into his own saddle, aware that his personal collection of hurts was not exactly minor. Sore saddle skin and lame muscles now had some bruises to go along with them. Lowry had hit him pretty hard on the arm and shoulder with that six-gun.

They pushed the horses to a run until they had covered one of the open stretches along the river. Then they eased down again, Kirby turning in the saddle to study the rear. There were two trails of dust now, the larger one that he knew represented the regrouping of the Cheyennes and another one, which seemed to be on the other side of the river.

"Looks like they've divided their forces," he told her. "Somebody's on our trail, but some of the others have headed north."

"Chasing Joe, perhaps?"

"No."

"How are you so certain?"

"Just take my word for it." He didn't want to tell her that he had been listening all the time to that yelling behind them. There had been no mistaking the shrill scream of triumph which told him that a Cheyenne had counted coup on a particularly hated enemy. That sound had carried to his ears above all of the other yelling which had indicated the confusion and anger of the Indians. He would never have to worry about Joe Lowry again.

Again there was a silence as they walked the horses, trying to keep the weary animals from collapse. It was Nell who broke it. "Did they?" she asked shortly.

He didn't pretend that he misunderstood. "They did," he told her. "And they're still not satisfied. I think that two or more of them are trying to run us down."

"Why should they? It was Joe they wanted. You told him that yourself."

"Which was the truth. But those Cheyennes are in a bad spot. All of them are Indians who have tried to keep the peace. That's why they determined to kill Lowry. The trouble is that for them to kill any white man—even one like Lowry—is sure to cause more hard feelings between the Indians and the authorities. We're witnesses. They can't afford to have witnesses."

"But we . . ." She broke off quickly. "I understand how they must be thinking."

"Let's trot a little more," he suggested, looking back again. "The main idea now is to keep ahead. We got a good jump while they were getting their gang together again—and doing their chore back there. We can't afford to lose the advantage."

He kept looking back as they made good time upstream, neither of them talking. The dust directly behind them was hard to read, but he felt pretty sure that only two or three of the Cheyennes had taken up the chase. What he couldn't explain was that other lot of dust across the river. Why had they cut across? There was no chance of their taking any short cut that would let them get ahead. Where were the rest of the Indians going?

They were still following the river, picking high or low ground along its course depending on which offered the best footing. As long as they could maintain the pace they would be all right; the Cheyennes behind them definitely had not gained on them.

When they eased the broncs after a brief run Nell asked abruptly, "Do you think they can catch us?"

"No."

"What makes you sound so sure?"

"It figures out that way. Those Indians were mostly old men and they must be pretty weary. I don't believe they can keep going long enough to run us to earth."

She uttered a mirthless little laugh. "And what makes you think that I can keep going long enough to prevent them from doing it? I'll bet there isn't an Indian in the whole band that feels any older than I do right now!"

He knew a quick remorse at the way he had shown so little consideration for the hardships she had been through. Necessity had made him ignore his own pains and fatigue, but he should have known that Nell didn't have the strength to take such a beating and not suffer from it. Still there would be no point in trying to coddle her now. She had to keep going.

"You don't look so old," he laughed, the laugh not quite coming out as cheery as he had planned it. "You're kinda dirty and bedraggled, but you don't look bad at all. Kinda cute, even."

"Don't try to butter me up! I know what I look like."

"How you feel is what counts. Stop feeling sorry for yourself and take account of stock. What's going to keep you from going right on to safety?"

"A lot of things." She kept her voice grim, but he had a feeling that even in talking about her troubles she was helping herself to overlook them. "First, I made a twenty-four-hour ride without any rest worth mentioning and almost no food. And practically at the point of a gun. After that I was struck in the face, knocked down, tied up, and left to get what sleep I could while I had cramps all over my body. I've been shoved around some more, shot at, and chased. The bruises from yesterday's ride are now overlapping the blisters I'm collecting from this one. How much do you think a poor widow woman can stand?"

"Plenty," he told her with a grin. "Anybody who can reel off a list of disasters like that is mad enough to do a lot of riding."

"But I hurt."

"Never mind; it doesn't show."

"So you think I'll keep going if you keep making me angry? Is that it? Well, mister, you're going at it in the right way!"

"Good. Now push that bronc again. I want to have a good lead on those redskins when we break out into the open beyond this next stand of timber. Maybe we can ease your blisters sooner than I had hoped."

She offered one retort as the horses were nagged into a renewed run. "Better forget that 'we' business when you talk about easing my blisters. This particular batch will have to be my own personal responsibility."

"Don't say I didn't offer my services," he shot back, content that she could make pretty personal jokes at such a time.

CHAPTER 16

He took a final look at the backtrail dust before they swung into the wooded area. Pursuers were still back there but they hadn't gained much. Maybe they hadn't gained at all. The other dust cloud had almost disappeared. A faint haze indicated where it might have been, but there was no sign that the other lot of Cheyennes had headed upriver on the other bank.

"I think we can do it," he told her as they took a more cautious pace through the timber. "I'm just guessing, but I think they detailed two or three warriors to run us down while the rest of them high-tail it back to the reservation."

"Why?"

"Same reason that they can't afford to have witnesses to this little mission of theirs. They're the peaceful branch of the government's little red wards. They want to keep that reputation. At a time of trouble they can't be having anybody missing them. Too many questions might be asked."

"I see. You think most of them are hurrying back to their proper places so no one will suspect that they have been gone."

"I don't see any other way to account for the way they left. It's a safe bet they're not chasing us any longer."

"But what of the ones who are?"

"Even Indians can be fooled. If I recall this piece of country, just ahead of us I think we can do it."

She groaned a little. "I hope you're right. If I don't get out of this saddle pretty soon the blisters will be so big that they'll ride and I'll have to walk."

"That's one thing I've always liked about a woman," he chuckled. "A knack of thinking beautiful thoughts."

"Shut up!"

"Don't be so bossy. People will think we're married."

"What people?"

"The ones we'll meet when we get back to civilization. By the way, maybe you'd better marry me. The blisters will be better soon."

"I ought to," she declared, half amused and half annoyed. "Just for spite."

"Motives don't matter. My idea in suggesting it wasn't very romantic, I'm afraid. It's just that I got to thinking how nice it would be to have you around. You're a real pretty gal when you have a decent chance to get fixed up. You don't get fussed very easy. You're tough enough to stand even me. And somehow I've had you on my mind most of the time lately. Must be you've made an impression."

"That's a gallant speech if I ever heard one.

I'd be very flattered—if I were 90 years old and half-witted."

He laughed. "That's exactly what I mean. Every inch a lady."

They were silent until the forest began to thin out again. Then Nell asked, "How much of what you said back there was serious?"

"Most of it. Serious ideas expressed in what didn't sound like very serious words."

"Then you really are asking me to marry you?"

"Not exactly. I'm warning you that if you don't I'll make a nuisance of myself for years to come. Of course I'd probably be a nuisance if you did."

She uttered a little laugh. It wasn't much of a laugh, but under the circumstances it sounded pretty good. "You're being honest anyway."

"Which is just one of my sterling qualities. Wait until I have a chance to show you all of them. I'm lazy. I snore. I don't shave any oftener than is absolutely necessary. I cuss a bit. I haven't had a steady job since I left the army." Then his voice took on a vast innocence as he added, "But I sing real good."

"How nice." She didn't make it anything but casually polite this time.

Again there was a period of silence. Kirby broke it by asking, "Will you?"

"Will I what?"

"Will you marry me?"

She turned to look straight at him, her

expression placid in spite of the dirt and bruise. "Of course I will. I simply wanted to hear you ask the question properly—without all the nonsense."

"Fair enough. I asked it. You answered it. Now let's get clear of those damned Cheyennes."

They moved out into open country again, Kirby keeping up a running fire of idle chatter. Partly he was talking to keep Nell from thinking about her aches and pains, but partly he just wanted to talk. A sort of nervous energy impelling him. He had felt it ever since he listened to that Cheyenne screeching over Lowry. The burden of years had been lifted from him. Present danger seemed puny by comparison to the load he had been carrying.

In a vague sort of way he supposed that he ought to feel cheated. Years of effort and grim planning, years of living an unnatural life had gone into that campaign of vengeance, but he had never managed to accomplish a single part of the job. The Cheyennes had beaten him to the final deed just as the Montana vigilantes and the New Mexico Apaches had handled the first two parts. As a vengeance seeker he had turned out to be a complete failure. And he was pretty elated about it.

They rode up over a slight rise and he had another chance to look back. The pursuers were still coming but they had lost considerable ground. Probably the old Indian was beginning to weaken. At least Kirby thought of it in that way, for some reason assuming that one of the warriors in the pursuit party would be the younger one. Any others would be old.

He studied the dust intently and spoke his mind. "Not to the stretch of timber yet. I think we can make it."

"Make what?" Nell wanted to know, rousing herself from the dogged silence which she had adopted while Kirby talked.

"We'll try to fool 'em. Can you swim?"

"A little. I didn't think the river was deep here."

"Holes," he explained shortly. "Follow me."

He turned his horse into the brown flood, noting that the water was a little higher than it had been on the previous day. Somewhere on the headwaters a summer storm had occurred. It suited his purpose exactly. The Indians would have no chance of finding hoof marks on sandy bottom with the water as muddy as this.

He sent the horse out to mid-stream, finding nothing in the way of depth, and then turned back downstream. Instantly Nell offered a protest. "We're going back!" she exclaimed. "What are you trying to do?"

"Good girl," he called back over his shoulder. "Still alert, I see."

"But we'll be . . ."

"Creek over there." He nodded toward the far

shore where cottonwoods and willows marked the mouth of a tributary. "A small cutback to throw them off the scent. Then we hide out."

She nodded, protesting no further.

Now the dust downstream seemed to be lessening, and he guessed that the Cheyennes had entered the stretch of woodland. For the next few minutes they would not be able to see the river. But it would only be a matter of minutes. Timing had to be good. Getting into the cover of those willows before the Indians could reach an observation point might prove to be a pretty tight fit.

It was almost too tight. Just before they reached the mouth of the smaller stream, Kirby felt his horse slip sideways and he realized instantly what it meant. The eddies formed by the two streams had built up a sand bar and had dug a deep channel just on the outside of it. He tried to warn Nell but it was too late. Her horse had plunged into the deep water and was being swirled downstream, Nell already out of the saddle and struggling to hold on.

"Stay with the horse," Kirby called to her. "Just keep your head out of water. I'll be with you in a jiffy."

For a few seconds neither of them could do anything except fight for some kind of control of the struggling horses, but then Nell took a dozen clumsy strokes and began to climb into shallower water. She still held the reins and her horse followed meekly enough. Kirby promptly followed suit, a little chagrined that he had not been able to help.

"Good girl," he told her hastily. "Stay afoot now and get into the creek without leaving any traces if you can."

She replied with the briefest of nods, picking a way along the edge of the creek's shallow channel. The water was clearer in the creek, a fact which Kirby didn't like at all. They were bound to roil it up somewhat and the Indians might notice if they came across to look.

Still there was nothing else to do. He followed as she led the way between the willows and up the creek, both of them keeping to the middle now where the bottom appeared to be pretty stony. A good hundred yards from the river, where the creek's banks were high and well screened by brush, he called a halt.

"I'm going back to watch," he told her. "You hold the horses right here. They'll be willing to stand still for a while."

He pulled his six-gun, wiping away the water and examining the cartridges in it. Two of them didn't seem to have the lead as tight as it ought to be, so he removed them and replaced them with tight shells from the belt. With any luck the gun would fire all right.

Nell tied both horses to projecting roots as

Kirby worked with the gun. "I'm going back with you," she announced.

"Better get some rest. You need it."

She shook her head, muddy water spraying from her hair with the motion. "Don't be foolish! Do you think I could rest if I didn't know what was happening?"

His smile was partly one of approval and partly wry amusement at the bedraggled picture she made. The meticulous Mrs. Helen Perry was certainly a sight no one at Fort Fetterman could ever have imagined. "Suit yourself," he told her with a chuckle. "You will anyway—and I suppose I might as well get used to having you around."

He started down the creek as he spoke, making the mistake of turning his head to show a smile with that last remark. It left him just enough off balance so that when he stumbled against a stone he could not save himself. He twisted wildly but sat down in water about two feet deep, keeping the gun high enough for it to remain dry but otherwise looking mighty awkward as he went under.

Nell promptly grabbed his arm and helped him to his feet, her tone one which she might have used toward a perverse small boy. "Next time save your lovely romantic remarks for a more appropriate occasion. I can't always be handy to get you out of the messes you blunder into."

He wiped the water from his eyes with the back of his forearm. "Score one for you," he acknowledged with a wet grin. "I'll be a good lad. Let's go."

It took only a minute or two to reach the mouth of the creek, the willows offering good concealment for their purpose. Kirby led the way into the thicket which fringed the upstream point of the junction, pushing through until they could look out over the river.

"Make yourself as comfortable as possible," he warned. "This could get pretty tedious."

She made a wry face and went flat, belly down in a patch of mud behind one of the willow clumps. "This is fine," she breathed. "It's the only position that won't bother my blisters. And I can see out beneath the branches."

He recalled how neat and particular she had always appeared. It had taken him a long time to realize that she wasn't really prim, fussy, and vain but was simply one of those women to whom personal care was a matter of accepted habit. He had never seen her look anything but perfectly groomed, but now she sprawled contentedly in the mud, bright hair showing its gold only on the very top of her head.

She seemed to read some of the meaning in his grin but smothered the words that started to come. Instead she whispered, "The Cheyennes!" With the Indians a good hundred yards distant the whisper was a little on the overcautious side but neither of them noticed.

Kirby answered in the same guarded tone. "Now we'll see what they try to do."

There were two of them, just as Kirby had figured. His guess also had been right in thinking that one would be the youngest warrior of the group. The older one was one of the chiefs who had insisted that no witness must be permitted to live. Kirby decided that if he had to kill either or both he would be just as well pleased that it should be this pair. He hoped no killing would be necessary. After all, the Indians had done a job for him as well as for the tribe.

"They might be tough," he told Nell. "The others hustle back to the reservation so they wouldn't be missed and get into any trouble. This pair is a bit more determined."

The Cheyennes halted at the spot where the refugees had taken to the water, arguing there for several minutes. Even at the distance it was pretty clear that the old chief wanted to keep right on up the river while the other fellow suspected a trick. Both of them must know that this had not been a simple fording of the river; there was no decent place to come out on the north shore and no easy passage through the hills.

But there was the creek. The younger warrior pointed to it several times while the two of them were making a futile search of the river itself, obviously trying to see marks on the bottom through that muddy water. Finally the younger one seemed to win his point and the pair turned downstream, following practically the course Kirby and Nell had taken. They were watching the willows closely, and Kirby held the six-gun ready in front of him, once more making certain that no mud would clog its action. Once they made their turn into the creek, he would have to kill both of them.

Then the old chief struck that sloping mud flat. He tried hard to keep his horse from going over but the animal stumbled and then slid, falling sideways to dump his rider into that tricky little channel. Evidently the old Indian could not swim for his younger companion promptly leaped into the water and went after him, the two Indians and both horses being swept downstream in a threshing tangle.

Nell whispered quickly. "I didn't make such a mess as that, did I?"

"Stop bragging. I'm proud of you, but you don't have to show off."

"More gallant speeches!" she sighed.

Then they watched silently as the Indians found footing below the riffle. The old man was sputtering and coughing but had come to no real harm. Still he was making it clear that he wanted no more of this kind of business. His companion captured both horses and came back to get his

247

elderly partner straightened out. He paused for a minute or two to stare speculatively into the mouth of the creek from a slight downstream angle, but both Kirby and Nell were well hidden. Kirby's glance told him that the creek water seemed to be flowing clear enough, and he guessed that the Cheyenne was seeing it that way also. At any rate the warrior seemed satisfied and motioned toward the shore they had left. The older man didn't waste any time in heading for it.

"That's that," Kirby said in the same cautious whisper. "I hope they don't have any lingering doubts."

They watched until the Cheyennes were lost to sight, far upstream and still on the opposite shore. "Maybe we're lucky," Kirby commented. "That younger man probably followed part of your sign coming out. He'll remember that you traveled in the water quite some distance. Maybe he'll figure it's going to be that way now."

She scrambled to her knees, glancing down ruefully at the muddy front of her dress. "Can we take time to clean up a little? Now that I've stopped being quite so scared, I realize how I must look."

He reached out to pull her toward him, finding it a little difficult to get a good grip. Then he kissed her soundly, unmindful of the taste of mud. "I never kissed a messier woman," he said.

"Nor a nicer one. Let's see what we can do about getting clear of this wallow."

By the time they had waded back to the waiting horses he had a plan. "I think this creek must be spring fed," he told her. "It's too clear to be just another wash. We'll find a place where you can wash your face—and tend your blisters. While you're doing it, I'll climb a hill and see if I can make sure what our recent visitors are doing. My guess is that they'll stay clear of us for some hours. It'll give us a chance to rest a bit. We could even find a bite to eat if you don't mind hard rations soaked in muddy water."

She shook her head tiredly. "I didn't even know I was hungry until you mentioned it. Now I think I could eat the mud itself."

"We'll do a little better than that. Come along."

CHAPTER 17

They led the ponies up the creek, staying in the water both to hide the trail and also because it felt good to splash along. Weariness made for slow progress but neither of them worried about that. With no pursuers behind them they didn't care about time. After twenty minutes of it they reached a larger growth of cottonwoods which circled a small pool. The water was not deep but was quite clear, and the bottom was sandy rather than muddy.

"This'll do," Kirby announced. "Find a place where you can be comfortable and I'll take care of the horses. Then I'll go see what our red friends are doing."

He put both horses on lead ropes so that they could reach both the grass and the water, keeping them downstream from the pool. Nell had already seated herself in the shallows and was trying to wash some of the mud out of her hair. He gave her a brief wave and climbed to higher ground.

The afternoon was waning rapidly and he found it difficult to stare into the declining sun. Finally, however, he saw the film of dust against the hot sky. The Cheyennes were still moving west.

He was about to return to the creek when he

realized that there was another trailer of dust up the river. For a moment or two he wondered whether the rest of the Indians had made some sort of miraculous detour, but then he remembered Truitt and the other soldiers. He had quite forgotten about them with all of the excitement of the past twenty-four hours, but now he knew that the second lot of dust must be theirs. They would have spent just about this amount of time in unraveling the trail tricks Lowry had set for them.

Shading his eyes against the glare he sat down to watch those dust clouds converging. It took a little while but then the pattern broke, the nearer dust fading away. When he got up again, it was farther to the north and Kirby could guess what it meant. The Cheyennes had seen the soldiers ahead of them and had forded the river to avoid them.

He moved to a higher knob a little farther away from the river and the picture became quite clear. He could see the tiny dark specks which would be riders making the dust. The two Cheyennes were high-tailing it for home. To them the four troopers coming down-river must have appeared as the advance guard for a substantial force. They were getting out while they could.

At first there were signs of a chase but then the old pattern of dust resumed. Truitt was sticking to his original job. He and his men were back at the task of following those tracks. Kirby chuckled and wondered what the sergeant would think when he found the newer sign.

He went back to the cottonwoods, making plenty of noise to advertise his coming. Nell was spreading her wet dress on a bush, her stockings already draped across a cottonwood limb. She wore only a wet petticoat which clung to every fine curve of her figure, but she greeted Kirby as though nothing unusual was to be noted.

"Are they still going west?"

"No. They've changed. Heading back to the reservation now." He noted that she had made a pretty good job of rinsing her hair, tying it back with what looked like a garter. "We can forget about them."

"Good. And stop staring at me like that!" Her tone didn't come out half as severe as she seemed to be trying to make it.

"Just staring in appreciation," he told her. "How are the blisters?"

"No blisters. Just chafes and bruises. And that's bad enough! Why did the Indians give up so suddenly?"

"Our mutual friend, Sergeant Truitt and his boys, I think. They set out from the Agency when I did, following the trail you and Lowry left. I gambled on a short cut."

She let that sink in. "And it has taken them until now to get here?"

"That's the way it looks. Lowry didn't make it easy, you know."

"I know." There was a shade of bitterness but then she broke away from it, her clear eyes intent upon Kirby. "Your guess saved me, didn't it? I'd have been dead by this time if you hadn't saved those extra hours."

He bowed formally. "In all modesty I can lay claim to having pulled a real smart move. You can show your appreciation any time at all."

She shivered a little and he knew that it wasn't the wet petticoat causing it. "Don't make jokes like that. I'm very grateful and I think you did a wonderfully smart thing. Although I suppose I'll spoil you by saying so."

"I'm pretty insufferable anyway," he reminded her. "What have you got to lose?"

She laughed at that. Then, abruptly, she asked, "Why didn't you kill Joe when you had him by the throat?"

"You asked me not to."

"But I asked you several times before that. You refused to call off your bloodhound campaign."

He dropped his pose. "I changed my mind about several things. For eight years I told myself that killing Joe Lowry—and the others—was the most important thing in the world to me. Lately I came to the conclusion that it wasn't as important as I'd made myself believe. If killing Joe Lowry meant losing you, then Joe would have to go on living. When I headed for Fort Robinson, I knew that Lowry was under arrest. I was quite willing to let the army handle his punishment."

He saw the uncertainty in her gaze and went on earnestly, "You must realize by this time that I didn't make this last chase to get Joe. I came to get you."

"How could I know that?"

"Ask yourself a few questions, serious questions." His smile came a little more easily as he added, "We can afford to be serious now. We don't have to make funny talk to keep from getting into a panic."

She nodded her understanding. "I supposed that was what you were doing with all of the nonsense. Thanks for helping me to keep going. . . . And I rather liked it. Now what about those questions? What am I supposed to ask?"

"Ask yourself why I let Lowry pick me up so easily? He wasn't that smart and I wasn't that stupid. Then ask yourself what was the meaning of those useless shells in my gun."

She thought it over and nodded once more. "You let him catch you and take a useless gun away from you so that you could jump him when he tried to use it. Was that the idea?"

"Partly. I knew that I was not going to have time to make the kind of attack I had planned. The Cheyennes had complicated things for me. I had no time to find the hiding place as I normally would have found it. They would have come up on me before I could manage it with any safety to myself. So I had to find a short way of getting to you. The shortest one seemed to be that of letting Joe bring me in. That's when I dumped the powder out of the shells."

"But the awful risk!" she exclaimed. "I know now that it would have been more like him to have shot you down than to have captured you." There was bitterness as well as concern in her voice as she said it. Any lingering affection she might have felt for her stepbrother was certainly gone now. And for ample reason.

"A chance I had to take," Kirby said shortly. "I couldn't think of any other way to get to you fast. I had to gamble that I would get a chance to pass the warning about the Cheyennes and that Joe would try to use me in some way for getting clear of them. Anyway it worked. Nothing else counts."

"It was still a terrible risk to run."

"I've run worse ones—for the sake of vengeance. I thought I could take a chance this time for a much better purpose."

"To rescue me?"

"Can you think of a better one? I told you that when I stopped figuring on vengeance as the biggest thing in my life it was because I'd found something that was bigger. Getting you was what I had in mind. If I couldn't get you out of that place, I didn't care very much whether I got out myself."

The tiredness no longer showed in the blue eyes as she looked squarely at him. "I apologize for what I said about your romantic speeches. After that one I can never utter another complaint."

He started toward her but pulled up again, looking down at his mud-caked clothing. "I'll wait," he said with a grin. "But look out for yourself when I get clean!"

"Start washing any time," she retorted.

"I can't do it yet, damn the luck. I've got to get back to the river and head off those troopers. No reason for them to go on chasing after nothing. Anyway, they might have some rations left."

She glanced down at her wet petticoat. "You will bring them here?"

"Probably. So get your dress on; I don't want them getting any of the ideas that have been occurring to me."

She blushed but not with any show of displeasure. "Stop leering at me!" she snapped, the show of anger not very convincing.

"I'll leer all I like, sweetheart, and you can't utter a word of complaint. You promised. Remember?"

She put on a show of resignation this time, and once more it didn't carry much authority. "Oh well, I suppose I'll become accustomed to it in time."

"It won't take long," he promised. "You're going to get lots of practice. I'll be back before long."

He was still grinning happily to himself as he swung out to the higher ground and headed toward the mouth of the creek. He was bone weary, wet, dirty, hungry, and a long way from either rest or food. He didn't have a thing to complain about.

Only minutes after he reached the river he saw the troopers coming over a small rise. A little shouting brought them across, and he gave them a quick résumé of the day's events before leading them up the creek toward the cottonwood grove. "We'll stay right here tonight," he concluded. "All of us can use the rest. Tomorrow we'd better go take a look around that hideout of Lowry's and then we'll head for the Agency. You men chased off the last Indians who had any ideas of causing trouble, so it looks like we're done out here."

They exchanged stories as they rode toward the spot where Nell was waiting. Truitt and his men had been delayed just as Kirby had suspected. Because they had had to stop during the night they were still reasonably fresh—and they were carrying ample supplies. In addition to the usual marching rations each man had brought canned goods in his slicker roll. At least the food problem was solved.

Kirby and Nell ate hard rations while the men

made camp, a fire giving both of them a chance to dry out the wet garments they were wearing. No one talked very much until necessities were out of the way, but then Nell told her story, making even some of the complications brief and to the point. It was evident that she was having trouble in keeping her eyes open long enough to complete the tale.

Her first mistake, she admitted, was that at her first visit to Lowry at the Agency lockup she had told him why she had been searching for him. She had even shown him the bank draft for him which she had carried for so long, expressing her vast disappointment in discovering that she had been trying so hard to do something for such a despicable character.

When he saw his opportunity to escape from the Agency, he wanted that draft. He forced her to go with him, making her collect her scanty baggage so that the draft would not be left behind. It was only when they were well away from Fort Robinson, however, that he tied her up for the first time and searched her belongings for the paper. Until that time he had shoved her along at gun point, threatening to shoot if she made a murmur.

He found the draft easily enough but discovered to his anger and dismay that she had taken the precaution of having it made out to herself. He had tried to bully her into endorsing it, but she had refused, understanding him all too well by that time.

"If I'd signed it," she said simply, "he'd have killed me right then and there. Keeping that draft unsigned was my only way of staying alive. He threatened all sorts of horrible things, but I knew that he didn't dare to stop long enough to carry out too many of them. He struck me several times but then we went on."

She told it almost numbly, as though relating a bad dream, but the facts were easily understood. Lowry had to keep running and he didn't dare leave Nell behind. He needed time to get away from possible pursuit so that he could try some of his proposed torture methods to get her signature on that bank draft. She could only go along, determined to be stubborn to the end because no other course was left to her.

When they reached the hideout and found that it had been raided, the whiskey barrels broken and dumped in the creek, Lowry's anger had been pretty vicious. The bruise on her cheek had come from that incident. Then he had tied her up and left her, evidently searching the surrounding area for some sign of his missing partner. Nell had a feeling that he must have found the remains of the other man for he seemed sick and shaken when he returned. He ignored her for the balance of the time, but she knew that he was prowling restlessly around the place, perhaps anticipating the Cheyenne move which had been actually in the making.

"I didn't realize how desperate my plight really was," she went on in that same detached voice which was partly due to exhaustion and partly a matter of delayed shock. "I knew that he might try torture at any moment, but I think I would have gone completely out of my mind if I'd known that the Cheyennes were about to take a hand."

"You had a rough time, all right," Kirby said, his voice sounding a trifle gruff as he tried to smother much more tender feelings. "Now you'd better get some of the sleep you've been needing. With four good men to keep watch I don't think either of us ought to be bothered by anything tonight."

He took a saddle blanket across to her, remembering that the nights could grow pretty chilly. She took it from him, smiling sleepily. "Don't go away," she said.

That suited him fine.

When daylight broke his heavy slumbers he knew that not all of his aches were from bruised places. One arm was numb because it had pillowed a tousled blonde head. He worked it free gingerly, substituting a corner of the blanket, and scrambled to his feet, working circulation back into the arm.

"Sorry," she murmured, not even opening her eyes. "It was nice though."

"Real nice," Sergeant Truitt's voice agreed from a short distance away. "Ah reckon as how this heah business didn't tuhn out so daggone bad afteh all."

Kirby crossed to the newly stirred fire, sniffing the pleasant odor of the coffee which had been boiling there. "Seems like my whole crazy vengeance scheme had a way of turning out profitably even if I never did manage to do a single thing I started out to do."

Truitt frowned. "How's that again? Ah guess Ah didn't heah about that."

"Likely not. You just heard the story from Mrs. Perry." Using that name for her suddenly seemed very strange to him. "The first time I went after those men I pretended to be a miner while I looked for them. I got lucky. The claim I staked kept me going for months, and then I sold it for $70,000. With the money I set up a freighting business to cover the next move when I traced Lowry to New Mexico. Again I got lucky. The freight line is still turning over a profit. I never got my man, but I made a profit each time."

"That include this whiskey business?" Truitt asked with a chuckle.

"Maybe even that. But I wasn't figuring that money was the profitable part of this deal."

Nell opened her eyes to give them each a swift smile. "What he means is that he regained some sanity. That's worth more than dollars."

"A matter of opinion," Kirby told her solemnly. "This new sanity will probably keep me in a mess the rest of my life. Already I've got a lame arm out of it—and I haven't even started yet."

"Sorry?" she asked.

"Go back to sleep and rest your blisters!" he growled, his grin not quite staying out of sight. "You'll have me saying things that the pure young ears of cavalrymen should not hear."

"Fine chance!" she scoffed. Her eyes had closed again and her face was expressionless as she added, "It takes a wet petticoat to get a nice speech out of you."

Truitt looked a little confused. Kirby suddenly came to a decision. "Sergeant," he said briskly, "I want you to take your men and follow the sign down the river until you find that hideout of Lowry's. Make sure of what happened to him—and to this partner of his. We'll have to have a full report, just in case Lieutenant Beckwith happens to want one."

Truitt stared, not quite knowing how much of this was serious. "You folks be all right without us?"

"We'll be fine," Kirby assured him. "The Indian danger is past, I'm sure. Even up along the Powder I'll lay a good bet that we don't have anything big happening from now on. The Sioux won their victories and won't want to try their luck any more. They won't be able to understand why the defeated pony soldiers don't run for home like those Cheyennes ran from us the other day. It'll take time but I think it's over. We'll be safe enough here. Leave us a ration or two and we won't need anything else but rest."

"Mebbe yo're raht," Truitt admitted, still clearly dubious about the whole thing.

"Of course I am. You boys just follow the tracks like I told you. Make sure that the Indians destroyed every bit of that illegal liquor. Then head straight northwest to the Agency. We'll meet you there."

The sergeant still hesitated. "Mah ohdehs, Mistah Kuhby. Ah'm supposed to see to it that the lady don't . . ."

Nell spoke again without opening her eyes. "The lady thinks she'll manage, Sergeant. Stop worrying."

Truitt's grin came slowly, but then it broadened into a grimace which eventually became a significant wink at Kirby. Without a word he turned to give his orders to his men with gestures. The four of them mounted and moved out without looking back. It must have seemed like the discreet thing to do.

Center Point Large Print
600 Brooks Road / PO Box 1
Thorndike, ME 04986-0001 USA

(207) 568-3717

US & Canada:
1 800 929-9108
www.centerpointlargeprint.com